At first Alexander thought he'd only imagined the faint knock on his door because he wanted her to come to him. It was only when he heard a second, louder knock that he responded.

"Come in," he called, his heart pounding a little faster.

His door opened and in the faint moonlight casting in through his windows he could see her silhouette in the doorway. "Did I wake you?" she asked.

"No, I'm not even close to being asleep," he replied. "Did you need something?" His voice sounded slightly hoarse to his own ears as blood rushed through his body.

"I need you."

Her voice sounded stark and his heart pressed painfully tight against his chest. "You've got me, Georgina. Whenever you need me, you've always had me."

She remained standing, as if weighing her options. "It's just for tonight, Alex. I'm using you. I'm only inviting myself into your bed for tonight, not back into your life in any meaningful way."

"So, you just want to take advantage of me for a single night," he said with a forced lightness.

"That's about the size of it," she replied.

"Then what are you waiting for?"

SCENE OF THE CRIME: BATON ROUGE

New York Times Bestselling Author
CARLA CASSIDY

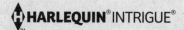 HARLEQUIN® INTRIGUE®

Recycling programs
for this product may
not exist in your area.

ISBN-13: 978-0-373-69791-5

SCENE OF THE CRIME: BATON ROUGE

Copyright © 2014 by Carla Bracale

This edition published by arrangement with Harlequin Books S.A.

For questions and comments about the quality of this book, please contact us at CustomerService@Harlequin.com.

® and TM are trademarks of Harlequin Enterprises Limited or its corporate affiliates. Trademarks indicated with ® are registered in the United States Patent and Trademark Office, the Canadian Intellectual Property Office and in other countries.

Printed in U.S.A.

ABOUT THE AUTHOR

New York Times bestselling author Carla Cassidy is an award-winning author who has written more than fifty novels for Harlequin. In 1995, she won Best Silhouette Romance from *RT Book Reviews* for *Anything for Danny*. In 1998, she also won a Career Achievement Award for Best Innovative Series from *RT Book Reviews*.

Carla believes the only thing better than curling up with a good book to read is sitting down at the computer with a good story to write. She's looking forward to writing many more books and bringing hours of pleasure to readers.

Books by Carla Cassidy

HARLEQUIN INTRIGUE

‡The Recovery Men

CAST OF CHARACTERS

Alexander Harkins—An FBI agent handed the task of a lifetime. He must not only lead a team to find missing fellow agents, but also keep his partner, his ex-wife, alive in the process.

Georgina Beaumont—An FBI agent who has spent her career trying to prove herself. She fears she's only an adequate agent and knows she was a terrible wife to Alexander. Now she has a chance to prove she can at least be a stellar agent and will take any risk necessary to prove it.

Nicholas Cutter—Had his ambition to be the best, most famous FBI profiler turned into something deadly?

Michelle Davison—An author who has showcased the missing FBI agents in her newest book. Had she gotten too close to her research?

Dr. Jacob Tanner—The professor taught about serial killers and the men who captured them. Was he doing some kind of sadistic homework after class?

Roger Cambridge—A young reporter who has his own internet news station and has followed all the previous cases. Is it possible he's creating the news in order to report it?

Chapter One

His heart jumped just a little when he saw her. Alexander Harkins wasn't really surprised. His heart had jumped the very first time that he'd met her, and now even two years after their divorce, it was as if it was an involuntary response that he had a feeling he would never be able to control.

Special Agent Georgina Beaumont might wear her rich dark hair boyishly short, but there was nothing remotely boyish about her large green eyes fringed with long dark lashes or her classically beautiful features.

There was definitely nothing faintly masculine about her full breasts, tiny waist and long slender legs. Even in a short-sleeved white blouse and neatly tailored black slacks, she managed to look effortlessly feminine and ridiculously hot.

He was seated on the other side of the large conference room when she entered and struck up a conversation with two other FBI agents who stood near the doorway.

Since their divorce, they'd worked out of this same building but hadn't been assigned a case to work together and had only run into each other occasionally.

The fact that they were both in this same room indicated that was about to change.

A knot tightened in Alexander's chest as he speculated on what they were all about to be handed. It didn't really take much thought on the matter. He knew the people in this room had been called together to form a task force to handle the issue of missing FBI agents and their loved ones.

He was more than happy to be part of the team because the last agent who had disappeared was a close friend of his.

Jackson Revannaugh had gone to Kansas City to work a case and had returned two weeks ago with a fellow FBI agent named Marjorie who had obviously won his heart. Three days ago Marjorie and Jackson had gone missing from Jackson's lavish apartment... just like an agent and her husband in Kansas City and another agent and his wife from the nearby small town of Bachelor Moon.

Two nights before their disappearance, Alexander had met Jackson and Marjorie for dinner at a restaurant known for its creole cuisine. He'd been charmed by Marjorie, who talked as if she intended to transfer from the Kansas City bureau to Baton Rouge in order to continue the relationship with Jackson. He'd never seen his friend, famous for being an unashamed ladies' man, so taken by a woman. Alexander had definitely heard the peal of wedding bells in the not-too-distant future for the two. And now they were gone, apparently taken from their bed in the middle of a Tuesday night.

There were eight agents in the room when Director Jason Miller entered. The tall, gray-haired man would be an imposing figure under any circumstances, but at the moment, with his strong jawline throbbing with tension and his blue eyes sharp and narrowed, he looked ready to breathe fire. The agents quickly found chairs at the long conference table and fell silent.

Alexander found himself seated across from Georgina. She cast him a quick smile and then directed her focus on her boss. That little smile of hers evoked old memories that he shouldn't have retained, that should have been erased the minute he'd signed the divorce papers two years before.

He quickly turned his attention to Director Miller, already dreading the job he feared was ahead of them all. On the wall behind Miller was a whiteboard / bulletin board that at the moment was covered with a large sheet of blank white paper.

The silence in the room shattered as Miller turned to the board and ripped off that paper. The whiteboard side was pristine, ready for dry-erase markers to get to work, but the bulletin board was papered with perfectly aligned photos of the missing people.

Alexander's heart squeezed tight as he looked at the photo of seven-year-old Macy Connelly and then moved to a picture of his dark-haired, handsome friend, Jackson. There were a total of seven pictures of people who had seemingly vanished from the face of the earth over the past couple of months.

These weren't ordinary people, four of them were seasoned FBI agents, one a respected sheriff, one a beloved wife and one a precious little girl. There was circumstantial evidence that they'd all been taken unwillingly from their homes.

"We have a problem," Miller said, his voice booming in the room. "We have seven missing people, no bodies, no ransom notes and you all are going to find out what has happened to these people. Officially, you are now a task force working solely on this case."

"Why here and not in Kansas City?" Alexander asked, knowing that two of the people had disappeared from the small town of Mystic Lake, just outside of Kansas City.

"Because this morning we believe we received communication from the perp." Miller moved to the board and tapped what was obviously a copy of a note that was pinned there. "For those of you who can't see from where you're seated, it reads, 'Right under your nose I work my plan, to become the best killer in the land. I've collected my research subjects two by two, and the world will shudder when I'm through.' It's signed by the FBI-trained serial killer." Miller looked disgusted.

Several of the other men muttered curses beneath their breaths and shifted in their seats. *Right under your nose*—that implied the perp was somewhere here in the Baton Rouge area. Alexander's stomach muscles knotted. *Research subjects*—that sounded like some crazy mad scientist who was taking apart the brains of his victims, he thought grimly.

As he listened to Miller give the condensed version of each of the crimes, he focused intently and tried to keep his gaze from the woman across the table.

He knew these particular crimes had stymied the law enforcement officials in Bachelor Moon, a small town not too far from Baton Rouge, and in Mystic Lake, Missouri. There had been no clues, no forensic evidence, nothing to indicate whether the vanished were dead or alive. The note, if it could be believed, at least indicated that the person responsible was someplace in this area... right under their noses.

Already adrenaline surged through him, the eagerness for the hunt and the anticipation of the chase. As one of the agents passed around thick folders to each of the people in the room, Alexander glanced up and his gaze met Georgina's.

Her green eyes appeared electrified and he knew she felt the same flood of energy, the readiness to get to work, that he did. He tried not to remember that her eyes had also lit up like that when they were making love.

They had been married for two years and the amount of information he knew about his ex-wife could be written on a small cocktail napkin.

He frowned and focused on the contents of the folder he'd been given. It was filled with the details and reports of the FBI agents who had originally investigated each event.

"Harkins," Miller said, the stern voice pulling Alexander from his reading.

"Sir?" he replied.

"I'm appointing you lead on this. Every agent will report to you, and you will report to me."

Dread mingled with the faint tease of potential redemption. The last time he'd taken lead on an important case, a young woman had been murdered a single minute before his team had arrived, and soon after that debacle, his marriage had failed.

He'd been plunged into a depression that had lasted for weeks, haunted by the face of the murdered woman and later enduring the pain on Georgina's face as she'd told him she needed out.

He knew he was a good agent, one of the best, and he also understood that his director was showing his complete faith in him by giving him the lead in a case of such importance.

"Thank you, sir," he replied. He stared down at the reports in front of him. Although he didn't have a marriage to lose this time around, he was intensely aware that seven people were depending on him doing the best job he possibly could to lead this task force to save them.

GEORGINA WAS ACUTELY AWARE of Alexander's presence from the moment she'd entered the conference room. He was a force of nature, emanating energy as his blue eyes focused on his surroundings.

Miller had left the room and Alexander had moved to take his place at the head of the conference table. He looked confident and at ease, but she knew him well enough to recognize how important this case was to him.

It was important to her as well. It was the biggest case she'd ever worked and, as the only woman in a roomful of men, she was desperate to prove that she was more than up to everyone's standards.

She'd spent her five-year career with the FBI trying to raise herself from being a good agent to a great one and this was the kind of case that could make that happen for her.

"We'll spend our first couple of hours here going over the contents of the folders and getting familiar with what's already happened and where we are now," Alexander said. "We'll start with what happened in Bachelor Moon."

She listened to his deep rich voice detail the fact that former FBI agent Sam Connelly, his wife Daniella and Daniella's seven-year-old daughter had disappeared during what had appeared to be a late-night snack session in their kitchen. Cookies and milk had been half consumed and a chair had been overturned, indicating that something untoward had occurred.

Although he looked calm and focused, she knew the torture he'd suffered the last time he'd been lead on a case that had gone bad. It had been a torment that had highlighted all her failings as a wife—as a person—and had ultimately forced her to make the decision that he was better off without her.

But that was then and this was now, she reminded herself. She couldn't dwell on the past, she needed to get her mind in this game, to prove she was as good as, if not better than, every other agent in the room.

"The second disappearance occurred in Mystic Lake, Missouri," Alexander continued. "Amberly Caldwell, an FBI agent, and her husband, Cole, the local sheriff disappeared from Cole's home. Our own Jackson Revannaugh was sent to Kansas City to help in that particular investigation. And then, as you all should know by now, three nights ago Jackson and his girlfriend, an FBI agent from Kansas City, went missing."

"How do we know that Jackson just didn't take his honey off somewhere for a few days?" Agent Nicholas Cutter asked. "He was on vacation for another week or so, wasn't he?"

"Yes, but according to the agents who investigated Jackson's house last night, all their identifications, their weapons and personal items were still in the bedroom where we assume they were sleeping," Alexander replied.

Georgina shot a glance at Nicholas. He was relatively new to the bureau and already had a reputation for being a hotshot wanting to make a name for himself. While she shared the same desire, she was a team player and she wasn't sure that Nicholas cared about any team.

She rarely made snap judgments about anyone, but the first time she'd met Nicholas Cutter, she hadn't particularly liked him. Still, she was a professional and never, ever let her personal feelings show. In her job this ability was a blessing. In her personal life it had been a curse.

"I want you all to take some time now and read through all the reports, look at all the photos that are included in your folders and familiarize yourself with everything that's been done so far with all the different law enforcement agencies that have been involved," Alexander said.

He returned to his seat across from her and the room fell silent except for the turning of pages as each of the agents began to learn the details of what had been accomplished through the different investigations and what was ahead of them.

Despite the fact that September had arrived on Wednesday, two days before, brilliant warm sunshine drifted into the windows and dust motes floated in the air.

Georgina was a fast reader and easily retained what

she read. She was finished long before the others and leaned back in her chair, hoping to escape the faint scent of Alexander that drifted across the table.

He wore the same spicy cologne he'd worn when they had been married. The scent of it stirred not only memories of being held in his arms, of making love, but also a depth of failure she had tried for two years to put behind her.

She looked back down at the folder and opened it to the photos of the victims. Failure was not an option now. She might not make friends easily, she might be incapable of any real intimacy with anyone, but she was going to work her butt off to find out what happened to these people.

"I think they're still alive," she said, breaking the silence that had filled the room. "We have no bodies, and the note, if it's really from the perp, implies he's keeping them as some sort of scientific study."

"I agree," Agent Tim Gardier replied. He was the youngest agent in the room. Painfully thin, with glasses and a head full of red hair that had probably not seen a barbershop in the last five years, he was also a genius computer geek and a genuinely nice guy.

"I don't know, maybe we just haven't stumbled on their bodies yet," Nicholas said.

Georgina mentally groaned. Just what they all needed, negativity at the very beginning of an investigation.

"It would be quite a challenge to house and feed seven captives," Agent Frank Webb added. "Especially if only one person is responsible for all this."

"It's too early in the investigation to make the assessment that we're only hunting one perpetrator," Alexander said. "What I hope is that the note received this morning really is from our man, and I hope it's the beginning of him becoming chatty."

"He hasn't had much to say until now," Nicholas said, a frown cutting across his broad forehead. "We don't even know if he's finished or if he intends to kidnap more people."

"You're right," Alexander said with a touch of impatience in his voice. "We don't know much of anything about this person. We don't know if he has enough 'research subjects.' We don't even know if his plans for more subjects include someone in this room."

These words sobered everyone. Their discussion lasted until one o'clock in the afternoon at which time Alexander called for a lunch break.

"Everyone back here at two o'clock sharp and I'll start breaking this down with assignments," he said.

Alexander was still seated in his chair with his focus on the contents of the folder as Georgina and the rest of the agents left the room.

She had no idea where the others were going, but she found herself walking next to Tim, who was obviously heading in the same direction as she was, to the cafeteria in the basement of the building.

"I have a feeling we'd better fuel up while we can," Tim said as they stepped into the elevator to ride down two floors. "I'm seeing long hours and few breaks in my future."

She gazed up at him, noting that the lights in the elevator turned his red hair into a furry ball of orange. "Have you worked with Alexander before?"

"Never as lead, but he has a reputation for being tough and driven. You should know how he works." The elevator stopped and the doors opened, and together they followed the hallway that would lead them to the cafeteria.

"He's definitely tough and driven," she replied.

Alexander had always been driven, it was part of what had attracted her to him in the first place. She could only imagine since the Gilmer case, which had gone wrong the last time he'd been lead investigator, that his drive for success was even deeper.

She grabbed a salad and Tim took two cheeseburgers and fries and they found a quiet table in the corner that suited them both. She knew Tim was comfortable with her, but like her, he wasn't necessarily a people person.

They ate quickly, not talking about the work ahead of them, but rather Tim explaining about a new computer program he was working on. Georgina found most of his talk gobbledygook, but she apparently nodded and murmured in the right places for he seemed pleased with both her and himself by the time they had finished their meal.

When they returned to the "war" room, Alexander was still in the same place he'd been when they'd left, letting her know he hadn't taken a lunch break.

She wasn't surprised. There had been many times during their marriage when they'd been working separate cases that she'd have to remind him to stop and eat or to fall into bed and catch a couple hours of sleep.

She knew how he worked. Without anyone in his life to tell him to slow down, he'd go until he crashed and burned. But he wasn't her worry anymore, she reminded herself.

She and Tim were followed into the room by most of the rest of the team. Nobody wanted to be the last one back from lunch.

The minute everyone was seated, Alexander once again went to the head of the table. "Right now we're all going to function on the supposition that the note we received is real, that our perp is holding these people and he's from the Baton Rouge area," he began. "I'm assigning Tim and Jeff to work on getting locations of all abandoned buildings and warehouses on the outskirts of town. If this person is holding seven people captive, then it would be in a place where nobody would see his activity and nobody could hear our victims scream." His jaw tightened.

Georgina's stomach clenched as she thought of seven people, including a little girl, yelling for help or shrieking with pain, from a place where nobody could hear them. Her determination to hunt and find, to capture and end this case, filled every cell in her body.

It was a familiar, welcome emotion, one where she dwelled most of the time. Work was her life…despite the dangers of being an FBI agent, it felt safer to her than personal relationships or friendships. She knew her failings and she did neither of those well.

"I want Nicholas and Frank to work on finding some sort of connection between all these missing people, besides the obvious that four of them were FBI agents," Alexander continued.

"Isn't that enough of a connection?" Frank asked as he raked a hand through his thinning gray hair.

"I don't think so. If that was the case, why would our perp go all the way to Mystic Lake? Why take somebody from Bachelor Moon? If all he wanted was random FBI agents, then he could have taken his pick from people who work right here. There has to be more of a connection. It feels to me like these people were specifically targeted, and we need to find out why."

"We'll get on it," Nicholas replied with a firm nod of his head.

Alexander looked at the last two male agents in the room. Terry Connors and Matt Campbell, both seasoned agents who were known for their attention to detail.

"I want you two to go over all the information we have from both the Bachelor Moon and the Mystic Lake disappearances and maybe your fresh eyes can see some detail, something that so far has been missed. You can travel to Bachelor Moon, but at this point, will interact with Mystic Lake authorities by phone or whatever. As we go along, if you need to travel there, we'll make arrangements."

Georgina tensed as she realized she was the only person in the room who hadn't been handed a specific assignment. Alexander's blue gaze met hers.

"Georgina, you'll be working with me, and we're going to start at Jackson Revannaugh's apartment and continue the investigation into his and Marjorie's disappearance."

She made sure her face revealed no emotion other than compliance, although she'd rather work with anyone on the team other than Alexander.

In the past two years they had managed to have very little interaction with each other and that had suited her just fine. Apparently he intended the two of them to work as partners within the task force.

I can do this, she told herself. She could remain professional and not tap into any memories that belonged to the two of them alone, memories that served only to remind her of what a pathetic life partner she had been.

There would always be a piece of her heart that would carry the Alexander brand, but it had nearly been buried now, and there was no digging it up, not that she thought he might want to.

All she wanted to do was find the bad guy and rescue the people who needed them. If working closely with Alexander helped her achieve that goal, then she was more than prepared for the challenge.

Chapter Two

It was nearly four o'clock when Georgina got into the passenger side of Alexander's company car. She buckled in as he slid behind the steering wheel, his energy a fierce entity that instantly filled the interior of the car.

He'd pulled on a lightweight black suit jacket that hid his shoulder holster and gun, but he still was a commanding presence without the show of firepower. She preferred a belt holster that she'd pulled on before they left.

"How have you been? I haven't seen you around for a couple of weeks," he said as he started the engine and then headed for the parking lot exit.

"Busy. I was working on the Browning fraud case. We managed to tie things up yesterday. Mr. Browning should be spending quite some time in prison."

"Chalk up another one for the good guys," he replied.

Georgina tried to relax against the seat, but it was difficult to find any relaxation at the moment. Her heart beat with a quickened rhythm. She assumed it was caused by the knowledge of the case she was now working and not how Alexander's familiar cologne filled the air.

"You met Jackson's new girlfriend?" she asked.

"I had dinner with the two of them last Sunday night, and then we were supposed to meet for drinks on Tuesday evening. When they didn't show and I still couldn't get hold of Jackson all day Wednesday, I knew in my gut that something was wrong. Last night, at my urging, Miller sent a couple of agents over to check on Jackson, and that's when they discovered they were gone, but all of their personal items were still there."

She saw the tightening of his fingers around the steering wheel and knew he had to be worried sick about Jackson's well-being. "What was she like? The woman from Kansas City?"

"She's Special Agent Marjorie Clinton." A hint of a smile curved his lips. "She's everything that Jackson isn't…she likes healthy food, she thinks he's full of baloney most of the time and it's obvious they are crazy in love."

"Jackson needs a good woman in his life," she replied.

"It appears he's found her." He frowned. "Now all we have to do is find them."

"It isn't possible they flew back to Kansas City if their identifications were left behind," she said, thinking out loud.

"They wouldn't have gone anywhere without his wallet and her purse, both of which were left at Jackson's place. And they definitely wouldn't have gone anyplace without their weapons."

"Any sign of a struggle in the bedroom?"

He shook his head, the late-afternoon sun gleaming on his black hair. "I haven't been to the scene, but according to the two agents who checked it out last night there were some bedcovers rustled, but no real sign of a violent struggle and, trust me, Jackson would have put up quite a fight. I'm hoping maybe you and I can find or see something they missed that might give us a clue."

"There weren't any clues found in Bachelor Moon or Mystic Lake," she replied.

A new knot of tension formed in his jaw. "Don't remind me." He pulled into the driveway of the luxury apartment complex where Jackson lived.

The Wingate apartments were set up more like condo units and definitely were for the wealthy who didn't want the responsibility that came with owning a home.

Jackson's unit was on the end of the last building in the complex, bumping up against a heavily wooded area and attached by a common courtyard entrance to the unit next door.

"Any sign of forced entry?" she asked as the car came to a halt.

"Not according to the initial walk-through." He cut the engine and turned to look at her, his blue eyes like hard-edged sapphires. "We either have a perp who is an expert at picking locks or, knowing Jackson, it's possible he went to bed without checking that all the doors were locked. He always thought he was invincible." Frustration deepened the tone of his voice.

"Then let's just hope that whatever has happened to him, he remains invincible," she replied.

He cast her a quicksilver smile that lingered only for a moment, just long enough to whisper heat through her. "Let's get inside and see what we can find." He opened his car door and was halfway to the courtyard entry as she hurried to catch up to him.

They had just reached the fence that led to the courtyard when a figure stepped out of the woods. Alexander filled his hand with his gun in the blink of an eye and then muttered a curse and jammed it back into his shoulder holster.

"Jeez, Joe, do you want to get yourself shot?"

FBI agent Joe Markum stepped closer to them with a wry grin. "Jeez, Harkins, are you trying to give me a heart attack?"

"You know my motto…shoot first and ask questions later," Alexander replied. "What are you doing out here?"

"I was assigned late last night to sit on the place to make sure nobody except appropriate officials gained access. Somebody should be arriving soon to take my place, but I'm assuming it isn't you two." He nodded to Georgina with a friendly smile.

"We're here to investigate," she said. "Miller formed a task force this morning and Alexander is leading it."

"And we're hoping to find something that was missed last night," Alexander said.

"Knock yourselves out." Joe gestured toward the front door. "It's unlocked and there's protective gear in boxes on the porch."

"Thanks," Alexander said and together he and Georgina walked through the gate and to the front door where a box of booties and latex gloves awaited whomever might venture into the house.

Georgina pulled on the protective gear and once again her heart began to beat faster. She'd never been in Jackson's home before, but it was the fact that she was about to enter what they'd already determined to be a crime scene that had her adrenaline flooding through her.

As she followed Alexander into the house, she tried not to notice how his lightweight suit jacket pulled over his broad shoulders, how his black slacks fit perfectly around his slim waist and down his long legs.

She tried not to remember what it had felt like to dance her fingers over his naked muscled chest, how her legs had often twined with his when they'd made love.

They had been great in the bedroom. It had only been when they got out of bed that she hadn't been able to get the relationship right. She firmly shoved these thoughts out of her mind as they entered Jackson's living room.

Jackson was the epitome of a Southern man and his furnishings reflected the style of warmth and invitation that would have done any Southerner proud.

The oversize sofa was a rich burgundy and gold print, flanked by burgundy wing-backed chairs. The coffee table was a large square of wood that held a gorgeous floral arrangement. The room was beautiful, but obviously rarely used and not the center of the home.

"Nothing looks like it's been touched in here," Alexander said as he moved into the next room, a large great room more casually decorated and obviously the space where Jackson spent much of his time.

A huge flat-screen television hung over a stone fireplace and two leather recliners provided the perfect places to sit and watch a movie or dancing flames. Again, it appeared as if nothing untoward had occurred in this room. There was no sign of a struggle or anything amiss.

Neither of them spoke as they entered the kitchen with its large table and variety of pots and pans hanging from a baker's rack on the wall. Everything was neat and tidy and she watched as Alexander dragged a hand through his dark hair.

"I guess the report we got that they were taken from their bed is true. Nothing seems to be out of place down here. We should head upstairs."

She nodded and once again found herself following him up the stairs that led to three bedrooms and two baths. The first two bedrooms and the hallway bathroom showed nothing untoward.

She felt her entire body tense as they approached the master bedroom. She stepped into the room just behind her partner. The king-size bed was unmade. The sheets trailed off to the floor on the closest side of the bed to the door.

"That bedding doesn't look normal to me," Alexander said as he stood still as a statue, his gaze lingering on the bed.

"By the way the sheets are hanging off, it looks like somebody was dragged from the bed," Georgina observed.

"I agree." The knot in his jaw throbbed as he pointed to the farthest nightstand. "But, how could anyone drag them out of bed when Jackson had his gun right next to him."

The gun was on the nightstand next to a silver-and-black lamp, an easy reach even in the darkness of night. "Maybe he drugged them? Drugged the food they ate before they came to bed? Slipped something in their drinks?" Her mind raced to make sense of the scene.

"I'll have the crime scene guys come back and check everything that's in the refrigerator to see if they find anything tainted by drugs."

He remained standing at the foot of the bed, staring at the room as if in a trance. Georgina did nothing to break his focus. She knew this was part of his process, this concentration that he used in an effort to see the crime as it happened, to understand any clues that might have been left behind.

She wondered if he still had nightmares. If somebody was seeing to it that he ate right. She'd heard no rumors that he was dating anyone, but that didn't mean he wasn't. He'd had two years to move on, and two years was a long time for a man to be alone, especially a man as vital, as alive as Alexander.

"Were the lights on or off?" He finally broke his trance and turned to look at her. "Do you remember from the report if the lights in here were off or on when the first agents arrived on scene?"

She frowned thoughtfully, trying to picture the initial report. "Off," she finally replied. "Jackson is a big man. If they were both somehow drugged, then how did our perp move their unconscious bodies from here to a waiting vehicle down the stairs and outside?"

Alexander looked closely at the carpeting around the bed where the covers trailed to the floor and then stepped out of the room and stared down the long hallway toward the staircase.

He turned back to Georgina, a deep frown cutting across his forehead. "I don't know."

"Maybe they weren't drugged at all," she said thoughtfully. "Maybe the perp just got the drop on them, appeared in the doorway with a gun pointed at Marjorie, making it impossible for Jackson to take a chance at grabbing his own gun."

"Maybe," he replied absently. "Let me take a look in the master bath to see if there's anything there and then let's get out of here."

He disappeared into the bathroom and Georgina felt his pain, his worry for his friend resonating in her heart. He'd been given a huge job, made all the more important because his good friend was now one of the missing.

The Gilmer case had given him nightmares and thrown him into a black hole that she feared he would never climb out of. If he was unsuccessful on this case, she feared it would completely and utterly destroy him.

"It's six-thirty, you want to stop by Nettie's and grab something to eat and talk about all the things we don't know about this case?" he asked Georgina when they were back in the car and headed away from Jackson's place. "I don't know about you, but I haven't eaten anything today except a bagel early this morning."

She hesitated only a moment before replying. "Sure, Nettie's sounds like a plan. Besides, if I say no, you probably won't eat anything tonight."

He smiled tightly. "I always did hate to eat alone."

The restaurant was a favorite place for the FBI agents to grab meals as it was only a block away from the building where they all worked. The prices were reasonable, the portions generous and the food was delicious.

He tried to fight against the discouragement that attempted to work its way into his psyche. He'd hoped to find something at Jackson's place, but given the fact that the other two crime scenes had yielded nothing in the way of clues, he shouldn't be surprised that nothing had been found there, either.

Reminding himself that he'd had the case less than twenty-four hours, he wanted to eat and then take the files he had on the previous cases home to study them all again.

Before they'd all left the office, he'd told the team to be in the war room at seven the next morning, even though it was Saturday. Weekends and holidays would have no meaning at all until this case was solved.

The fact that nobody from the team had contacted him while he and Georgina had been gone meant none of them had anything to report. Hopefully by morning that would change.

They remained silent on the rest of the drive to the restaurant. He knew it was probably a mistake partnering himself with Georgina, given their history. He also knew how bright, how dedicated she was to the job, and that because of her knowledge of him and his habits, she'd make the perfect partner.

He pulled into the crowded parking lot. Nettie's on a Friday night was busy, but he hoped that he and Georgina could grab a booth in the back where they could talk in relative privacy.

Nettie's had an identity issue. While the food was more along the lines of home cooking, the interior was dim, with candles lit at each table as if it was pretending to be a fine-dining place.

Nettie greeted them at the door with a wide smile.

"Two of my favorite agents," she said. She was a testament to the good food she served. Short and wide with brassy red hair, it was rumored that she'd once scared away a young would-be thief by wielding a large wooden spoon and threatening to spank his ass clean off his body with it.

As Alexander had hoped, she led them to a booth in the back of the restaurant where the noise of the other diners was less audible and he and Georgina would be able to talk without shouting.

The moment they slid into the booth across from each other with the candlelight glowing on Georgina's face, a sense of déjà vu struck him and brought with it a sense of loss he'd never quite recovered from.

They'd eaten out often during the early days of their marriage in places where candlelight had bathed her beauty in a golden glow. At those times her eyes had glimmered with a love that had showered him with warmth.

Now that glimmer was gone and in its place was the pleasant but focused gaze of professionalism. *As it should be,* he reminded himself.

The waitress arrived with menus and to take drink orders. Georgina went with a Cobb salad while he ordered a steak and baked potato. They each ordered a glass of wine.

"This is going to be a tough one," Georgina said. "FBI agents in two different locations haven't come up with any clues to help apprehend or identify a suspect."

"True, but we possibly have something they didn't have," he replied.

"The note."

"Exactly. If it's the real deal, then we have the first communication from the unsub and I'm hoping it won't be the last."

She unfurled the cloth napkin to reveal her silverware and placed the napkin in her lap as the waitress arrived with their wine. "I don't want to be negative, but you know it's possible that note is from some crackpot, or that single note will be all we get from him," she replied once the waitress had left the table.

"I know, but I've got a gut feeling that this guy is the real deal and at a place where he wants to crow about his victories."

She smiled. "Rumor has it that your gut is rarely wrong. It will be interesting to see if he makes any more contact with us."

They sipped their wine, falling into a silence that he'd often experienced when married to Georgina. She'd never been good at small talk, as if afraid she might somehow give away a piece of herself she could never get back.

"How's life treating you?" he asked, perversely forcing the small talk issue while they waited for their meals to be delivered.

"Fine. I spend most of my time at work, which is how I like it."

"Are you seeing anyone?"

She raised one of her dark eyebrows wryly. "I don't have time to see anyone, and in any case I'm not looking for a relationship. What about you?"

He shook his head. "There's nobody in my life. Like you, I work so much it's hard to even think about starting a relationship with anyone."

He didn't say it aloud, but the truth was that the woman across the table from him had burned him so badly he had no interest in getting close to the fire ever again.

"I have a feeling we're all going to be putting in a lot of hours with this one," she said, deftly turning the subject back to work issues.

"I can't help but think that somehow there's a connection between the victims…the FBI agents who were taken. It has to be a connection beyond the fact that they were FBI agents—perhaps their specific expertise—otherwise why take Sam Connelly from Bachelor Moon? Why go all the way to Missouri to snatch Agent Amberly Caldwell and then come back here to take Jackson?"

"So, you believe the people who were taken with the agents weren't just collateral damage?" she asked.

The conversation halted as the waitress appeared with their dinners. Alexander waited until she'd moved away once again and then replied, "They could be some sort of leverage. There's no better way to get a man to talk than to threaten his wife or his child."

"But, Sam was a retired agent. He hadn't worked actively as an agent for some time," Georgina reminded him.

"True, but he left the agency with the reputation of being one of the best profilers in the country."

Georgina took a bite of her salad, a tiny frown of concentration dancing across her forehead. "Is it possible that somehow Sam, Jackson and Amberly all worked a case together?"

"Sam and Jackson might have worked together in

the past, but I can't imagine how Amberly figures in. She wouldn't have been a part of any investigations that Sam and Jackson might have worked here in Louisiana."

"Even peripherally?"

He gazed at her thoughtfully. "I don't know. That's definitely something we should check out. We need to find out about any cases Sam and Jackson might have worked together and how, if at all, Amberly might figure in."

"Maybe Nicholas and Frank will have something for us tomorrow morning," she said.

"The sooner the better," he replied.

They fell quiet as they focused on their meals. Alexander found himself remembering all the silences that had filled the two years of their marriage.

For the first six months or so, Alexander hadn't noticed it. Captivated by her passion, eager to share who he was as a man, what he wanted for their future, he'd talked enough for both of them. He'd been crazy in love with her and thought she'd felt the same.

It was only after she'd left that he realized the marriage had been a one-sided disaster. They were great in bed, they could talk late into the night about the cases they were working on, but when the conversation turned personal she grew silent.

He knew her parents were alive and that she had two older sisters, but she was estranged from all of them. She never told him what had caused the estrangement, in fact had told him she rarely thought about her family.

She knew everything about his childhood, but he knew nothing about hers. She'd been adept at changing the subject when the conversation got too personal and he'd been too crazy about her to mind.

When he'd decided to partner with her on this case, he'd thought he was choosing her because he knew her work ethic matched his own and he believed she was one of the brightest agents on the team.

Now, as he gazed at her across the candlelit table, he wondered if there wasn't more to his decision. Perhaps he not only wanted her by his side to help in the investigation, but maybe he was also hoping that by spending more time with her, he would finally unlock the mystery of Georgina.

Chapter Three

Georgina awoke the next morning just after five-thirty, her mind already whirling with the horror of the nightmare that had plagued her for years.

The dream was always the same. She was in a dark, small space, her stomach growling with hunger as the scent of food drifted in the air. No matter how hard she tried, she couldn't escape the dark place except by awakening.

Never one to linger in bed, by the time six o'clock arrived she was showered and dressed and in the kitchen waiting for the coffee to quit brewing.

She had thirty minutes to relax until she'd have to leave to get to the FBI offices by seven. Minutes later she sat at her table with a cup of the fresh brew in hand. As she played over the events of the day before, the last thing she could find was any kind of relaxation.

Already she felt tension riding her shoulders, a knot of anxiety in the pit of her stomach. It was bad enough that they had a complicated case where they didn't even know if the kidnapped victims were dead or alive.

As the only woman on the task force, she felt extreme pressure to overachieve, to prove herself to be the best that she could be.

It didn't help that Alexander had chosen to partner up with her. He reminded her of her biggest failure, not as an agent, but as a woman. She couldn't imagine why he would make the choice he did when he could have partnered her with any other member of the task force.

She sipped her coffee and stared out the window to the tiny fenced-in backyard. She had bought this small house three months after her divorce. It had been a bargain buy, as the place had been on the market for two years.

The Realtor who had sold it to her had explained that the small size of the two-bedroom house made it unappealing to any couple planning for a family or any family looking for a home.

It was perfect for Georgina, who knew there would never be a man in her life again, who knew there would never be any children. The spare bedroom was now an office, and she'd done little to decorate other than buying utilitarian furniture and hanging a couple of cheap landscape pictures on the walls.

She took another drink of her coffee and thought of the seven missing people and the note that had been sent to headquarters. If it was real, then it held a hint of crowing, of an ego that needed to be heard.

She could only hope that the ego needed constant feeding and the perp would maintain contact. It was often through some sort of communication that they got clues and found leads to follow in difficult cases.

At exactly six-thirty she left her small house and headed into work. Although it was only a fifteen-minute drive, she'd rather be a little early than late.

As she drove, she carefully kept her thoughts away

from Alex. She had no idea how the past two years might have changed him and didn't want to remember the man he'd been when she'd walked out on him.

She'd have to walk a fine line to remain strictly on a partner level and not allow herself to fall into anything personal. She couldn't emotionally afford to make a second mistake where he was concerned.

The Baton Rouge FBI field office was located in an unassuming two-story building nestled between a dry cleaning store and a bank. She drove around to the back of the building where there was a large parking lot and pulled into one of the empty spaces. She grabbed the file folder that had kept her up reading reports and looking at photos far too late the night before, and then left her car.

The sultry morning air pressed oppressively against her chest. Or was it just the anxiety of the case and the uncertainty of working closely with her ex-husband?

The bottom floor of the building was dedicated to computer rooms and bookkeeping; the basement held storage and a cafeteria. It was on the second floor that agents actively worked at their own desks.

This morning she passed by her neat and tidy desk to head down the hallway to the conference room that now housed the task force. The scent of fresh coffee greeted her as she stepped into the room, finding Alex and Nicholas Cutter already there.

A large coffeepot had been set up on a side table, along with several boxes of doughnuts. The cliché of law enforcement at all levels. But Georgina knew as well as anyone that the sugar rush of a doughnut and the caffeine of a hot cup of coffee often provided the energy needed to get through long hours.

She smiled at the two men as she entered and sat in the same chair she'd sat in the day before. While Nicholas looked energized and eager, Alex's face wore the faint lines of fatigue. Like her, he'd probably been up most of the night going over the files of the previous kidnappings.

Before either of the two men had a chance to greet her, other members of the team began to arrive and soon the room was full. Once they'd all found seats, Alex eyed them with a weary resignation. "How many of you saw the news this morning that broke the story that a seven-man, one-woman task force had been formed to investigate the disappearances of FBI agents?"

"I saw it and I'd like to know who leaked it," Frank said irritably. "We hadn't had much publicity about these disappearances until now."

"At least it didn't list our names," Jeff said.

"You know any reporter worth his salt will have our names by the end of the day," Nicholas added.

"If I find out anyone in this room leaked anything to the press, I'll have your job." Alex's voice didn't hold a threat, but rather held a determined promise. "Now, let's get to the updates."

The first came from Tim and Jeff, who had spent the day before with both paper maps and working on the internet to locate vacant buildings that were isolated enough for seven people to be held captive.

"There's dozens of places," Tim said. "There are abandoned warehouses and old factories all over the surrounding areas and within the city."

"We're making a list of addresses and working through city records to find out owner names," Jeff said. "But it's going to take at least a week or two for us to get them all and even then there might be some places that slip through the cracks."

"I'll check with Director Miller and see if we can get some help from the local authorities to physically check out the places on the list you're compiling," Alexander said.

It wasn't unusual for the FBI to occasionally work with the Baton Rouge Police Department when it came to a job too big for the agents to handle alone. The police would be able to cruise by the buildings and check them out in person, lightening the manpower needed for the actual footwork of the investigative end of things for the FBI.

Despite the tired lines that creased his forehead and made the small wrinkles around his eyes look deeper, Georgina couldn't help but notice that Alex hadn't changed much in the two years they'd been apart. His shoulders were just as broad, his stomach as flat and the air of command that emanated from him came naturally.

He was born to lead, and if it hadn't been for the Gilmer case, he would have led most of the difficult investigations that had come along in the past couple of years. She knew he'd been asked to be lead in other cases but had declined, indicating a lack of faith in himself. She was glad he'd finally decided to step up once again.

There was no question that if she allowed it, she would be attracted to him again. All the qualities that she'd fallen in love with in the first place he still possessed. But she couldn't allow it and besides, he'd given no indication that he wanted it.

Although there had been little change in him physically in the last two years, she had no idea what changes had occurred on the inside. The one thing she knew for sure was that nothing had changed her. She'd been wrong for him then and she'd be wrong for him again.

She tightened her fingers around the pen she held, telling herself it was vital she maintain her objectivity where he was concerned. Alex was nothing more than her partner, her immediate boss, and that's the way it would stay for as long as they knew each other.

When Jeff and Tim had finished their report, Alex moved on to Nicholas and Frank. "We've got nothing," Frank said, his brown eyes dark with frustration. "We went through social media, used Google on all the names of the missing people, used Google on the FBI agents, and nothing popped up to tie them together other than the fact that they are all agents."

"Actually, I found something," Nicholas said, a touch of smugness in his voice as his partner looked at him in obvious surprise. "There's an author who has a new book out and the book includes sections about Sam Connelly, Amberly Caldwell and Jackson."

A touch of new disdain swept through Georgina. It was obvious Nicholas had blindsided his partner, kept the information to himself so that he would get all the glory of the find. Nicholas Cutter was definitely not a team player and that was a big strike against him as far as Georgina was concerned.

"Continue," Alexander's voice was like a gunshot in the room.

"The author's name is Michelle Davison and the book is titled *Heinous Crimes / Men of Honor.*" Nicholas sat up straighter in his chair, obviously pleased to be the center of attention. "She has a section about Sam Connelly, who was head investigator when four children were kidnapped and he successfully recovered them. Amberly Caldwell is showcased for her work on what was called the Dream Catcher murders in Mystic Lake. She also has the details of the case Jackson worked a year ago...the Twilight Killer."

As much as Georgina hated Nicholas's showboating, his information sent a rush of excitement through her. This was the first definitive tie they'd found among the three.

"Do we have an address for Michelle Davison?" Alexander asked.

"She lives in New Orleans, but I spoke to her literary agent last night and Michelle is set up to have a book signing right here at the Baton Rouge College bookstore at seven tonight," Nicholas said.

"Georgina and I will attend the book signing and do an initial interview with her," Alexander said, ignoring how Nicholas's smile fell into a pouty frown. He'd obviously hoped to do the interview himself.

One of the agents had moved a box of doughnuts into the center of the table and Frank reached for one. "I don't see how a woman writer could have anything to do with kidnapping seven people. There's no way I believe we're dealing with a female perp." He took a bite of his doughnut and grabbed a napkin as raspberry filling fell down his chin.

"We all have to keep an open mind," Nicholas said.

"At this point we can't know if the perp is male or female or even a team. We just don't have enough information to make that call."

"That's right," Alex answered. "Matt and Terry, anything new on your end?"

"Not yet," Matt replied. "But we're digging for anything we can find."

As he continued to reaffirm assignments for the day, Georgina was already eager for the night to come. This was their first real lead and she couldn't wait for them to follow it.

"Nicholas, get me everything you can on Michelle Davison by noon. Frank, continue to look for other connections between the missing people. Georgina, you and I are going to get the files of the cases that this author showcased in her book and see if we can figure out exactly why she chose these particular cases, these particular agents to write about."

Georgina nodded. Catching a killer was rarely like it was shown on television, with high-speed chases and shoot-outs in dark alleys.

So much of the work to catch a killer took place in chairs, researching the victims' lives, going through reports until you were nearly blind, searching the web for something, anything, that might burp up a clue.

Granted, they didn't know if this particular unsub was a killer or not, but he or she was definitely a serial kidnapper and these cases would be investigated as if they were chasing a killer.

Her gaze drifted up to the bulletin board where the victims' photos remained. Her focus was drawn to the little girl who had vanished with her parents.

Of all the people showcased on the board, Macy Connelly would be the most expendable. The seven-year-old would be of no use to the kidnapper, especially a kidnapper who claimed to be an FBI-trained serial killer.

Georgina had always loved children, but even when she'd been married she had never envisioned having any of her own. She knew what she was capable of giving and it had never been enough to be a mother.

Still, there was something that haunted her about Macy Connelly, an emotion that skewered deep into her soul. It was as if Macy might have been the daughter she and Alex would have had if Georgina had been different, if she had been whole.

She could only hope and pray that they could solve this case before something tragic happened to the agents and their spouses, before something tragic happened to the blond-haired, blue-eyed little angel who appeared to be personally pleading with Georgina for help.

THAT EVENING AT SIX-THIRTY when Alexander pulled into Georgina's driveway and she stepped out on the porch, he was immediately sorry that he'd told her not to dress like an FBI agent, but rather as a woman attending a social function.

She walked toward the car clad in a short, green dress that he recognized as the dress she'd worn on their second date. The only difference was that she'd added a gold belt around the fitted waist.

Didn't she buy new clothes? Did she even remember that the green dress had been one of his favorites? Probably not. Georgina wasn't particularly sentimental. She was pragmatic and dealt only in the present.

In the brief time he'd been her husband he'd realized she didn't dwell on the past and she rarely looked to the future. She was always in the here and now, and there had been times during their marriage it had made him slightly crazy.

She opened the passenger door and slid in, gold hoop earrings dancing on her ears as the familiar scent of her perfume filled the air. She exuded a thrumming energy as she greeted him and then buckled her seat belt.

"You look nice," he said as he backed out of her driveway.

"Thanks, so do you."

He didn't look all that different from what he looked like every day. The only difference was his black slacks were paired with a black-and-blue pin-striped shirt instead of the regular white dress shirt. His blazer was the same one that had been slung across the back of a chair for most of the day.

"I'm so excited," she continued. "We've only been at it for a day and already a lead has come to light."

"We don't know how good this lead might be," he replied in an attempt to temper her enthusiasm. "The odds that we're going to solve these crimes tonight by attending a college bookstore autographing session are pretty minimal."

"True, but at least it's a place to start." She shifted positions to face him more fully. "We'll solve this one, Alex. We'll solve it and save every single one of those people."

The diminutive use of his name felt both familiar and intimate and he shoved away the wave of warmth that suffused him as he heard it. She was the only person in his life who had called him Alex. Both professionally and personally he'd always been Alexander.

"We're a long way from a solve, but I hope your optimism plays out," he said gruffly.

Damn her green dress and her use of Alex. The last thing he needed was to get lost in memories, in questions from the past that would splinter his attention. He needed to remain focused on the case and nothing else.

The Baton Rouge College campus was both huge and beautiful. Stately stone buildings were linked together by tree-lined sidewalks, and courtyards with benches invited students to gather for impromptu study sessions or social activities.

The bookstore was along a side street, and Alexander was surprised to discover the parking lot next to it full. He found an open curbside space about a block away and he and Georgina got out of the car to walk in the sultry evening air. "Feels more like early August than September," Alexander said.

"It is warm. Looks like she's drawn quite a crowd," Georgina said.

"Murder and mayhem always sell well," Alexander replied with a touch of disgust.

Georgina shot him a quick smile. "You can't blame people for being interested in the same things we are. If the readers who buy these kinds of books are freaks, then that makes you and me super freaks."

Alexander laughed, knowing that she was right. Neither of them would be where they were if they weren't drawn to the dark side of humanity.

He fought the impulse to place his hand at the center of her back as they walked side by side, as he used to do. It had always been a proprietary touch and he hadn't had that right for two years.

Focus, he thought as they entered the door to the busy bookstore. This job was his chance to stanch the nightmares of failure that played over and over again in his head. He was haunted by a single dead young woman; he couldn't imagine seven people haunting him if he didn't get this job done right.

Alexander estimated Michelle Davison to be in her mid-thirties. She was an attractive blonde with blue eyes and appeared to be greeting her fans with genuine warmth and friendliness.

There was a long line before her, and as he and Georgina fell into the line, he also noted the man who stood just behind the table where Michelle sat.

Tall and muscular, although he was neatly dressed in slacks and a short-sleeved white shirt, he looked like a thug. A tattoo rode the side of his neck and others crept up his muscled arms. Boyfriend? Bodyguard? Partner in crime?

Alexander couldn't help the suppositions that raced through his mind. His plan was to buy a book, chat like a customer and then once the signing was over have a more in-depth discussion with the author.

"I didn't expect this kind of crowd," he said, leaning closer to Georgina.

"I checked her out before you picked me up. This is her fifth crime book and she's grown quite popular," Georgina replied. "You think the guy behind her is her agent?" she asked dryly.

Alexander flashed a tight smile. "I've heard that

literary agents are tough, especially those from New York City."

A small laugh escaped Georgina and the sound pooled warmth in the pit of his stomach. It had been over two years since he'd heard the sound of her husky laugh.

He averted his gaze from her and instead focused on the other people inside the store. It was possible the very man they sought was right here in the room, eager to buy a book about the people he'd kidnapped.

Or perhaps Michelle took her research to a whole new level and she and the mountain man behind her were responsible for the disappearances of the FBI agents. It would make one hell of a publicity stunt.

His stomach knotted. Could that be what this was all about? Surely not. He hadn't seen any publicity concerning the missing FBI agents and the book that was being sold. The various departments involved had been playing the details of each case close to their vests.

As far as Alexander knew, no reporter had tied them all together to come up with a serial kidnapper at work. Until this morning, when it was reported that a task force had been formed. He'd like to get his hands around the neck of whoever had leaked that information.

He glanced at Georgina and noticed that she was perusing the crowd with narrowed eyes. She was probably thinking the same thing he was, that the perp might very well be right here in this room, eager to buy a book about the people he held captive. Hopefully the author they were about to meet would have some answers.

He breathed a sigh of relief as finally there was only one person in line before they'd be at the author's table.

"Professor Tanner," Michelle greeted the man in front of them warmly. "I can't believe you're here."

"Now, how could I miss such a special event for one of my best students?" the tall, well-built man replied.

"You're part of the reason I'm where I am," Michelle said as she signed a book for him. "Your classes were always so fascinating."

"Thank you. Let's hope there continue to be plenty of students who enjoy my classes." He took the book she'd signed for him and then Alexander and Georgina stood before the author's table.

"Hello, would one or both of you like a book autographed?" Michelle asked with a bright smile.

"I'd like one," Georgina said. "You can just sign it to Georgina."

"And we'd both like to have a little chat with you when this is all over this evening." Alexander pulled his official identification from his pocket and placed it on the table. *To hell with the idea of pretending to be a fan,* he thought. He just wanted to cut to the chase.

Michelle looked at it and then at him with a faint alarm on her pretty features. Alexander quickly tucked his identification away.

"Can we talk someplace other than here?" she asked. "I'd rather not have any of my readers know that the FBI is questioning me about anything."

"There's a coffee shop about three blocks from here at the corner of Magnolia and Mission Road," he said.

She nodded. "I know the place." She glanced at her wristwatch. "I'll be here for another half an hour or so. Shall we meet there in about an hour?"

She appeared curious and a bit apprehensive, but not

particularly scared or guilty. Alexander was eager to question her and find out what, if any, role she might have played in the crimes. "Make sure you're there. Otherwise we'll find you someplace where it might be less private."

"I'll be there," she replied, her lips morphing into a thin line as she turned her attention to Georgina. "Did you really want a book?"

"Yes."

Michelle quickly signed the book and handed it to Georgina. "I hope you enjoy it," she said as if by rote.

The two of them left the table, paid for the book and then exited the still-busy bookstore. It wasn't until they were back in Alexander's car and headed to the coffee shop that Georgina spoke.

"So, thoughts?" she asked.

"I have several. My first thought is what a great publicity stunt it would be for the three agents she wrote about in her book to suddenly go missing."

He felt Georgina's gaze lingering on him, could almost hear the wheels churning in her head. "It would be a great publicity stunt, but there's been nothing in the news until this morning to let people know that we've determined that the missing FBI agents are tied together."

"Odd, though, that the news broke on the morning of her book signing." He glanced over to her, noting how pretty she looked in the faint glow of the dashboard lights.

"Odd, or coincidental," she agreed. "Nobody in the crowd caught my eye as looking particularly suspicious. Even Michelle didn't look overly worried or guilty when you showed her your identification and said we needed to talk to her."

"I guess we'll have a better feel for her after questioning her," he replied as they pulled up in front of the coffee shop.

They grabbed one of the tall tables in the back where they would have a little more privacy, although there were few people in the place. Most of the college students would frequent the coffee shop throughout the day, but on a Saturday night they would all have better places to be.

"Sit tight. I'll go get us some coffee," he said. She sat on one of the tall stools and opened the book she'd bought as he headed for the counter.

"I'd like a medium black coffee and a medium caffe mocha, hold the whipped cream." He was vaguely surprised that what had been Georgina's favorite drink rolled effortlessly off his tongue after all this time. He wasn't even sure if she still drank what he'd just ordered for her.

He paid for the drinks and grabbed them, and as he turned to face her, he immediately knew something was horribly wrong. She had her cell phone at her ear.

Her face was the pale shade of death, but her eyes were huge and darted at him frantically. He raced to the table at the same time she set her cell phone down with a hand that visibly shook.

"Georgina, what happened? Who was on the phone?" He set the cups down and reached for her hand. Her icy-cold fingers grabbed onto his and held tight.

"It was him." Her voice whispered from her. "He said he was the person we were hunting." She drew a deep breath, some of the color returning to her cheeks as she disengaged her hand from his and instead curled her fingers around the warm cup in front of her.

"Are you sure it wasn't some sort of a prank phone call?" he asked.

Her green eyes held a faint tinge of fear as she slowly shook her head. "He said he'd be in touch again and that Macy told me to get a good night's sleep, that I was going to need my rest if I was going to save her."

Myriad emotions rose up inside Alexander, questions about if the call had really come from the man they sought and when he might make contact again. More importantly, why out of all the task force members had he connected with Georgina? His stomach clenched tight.

Did this mean that Georgina was in danger?

Chapter Four

Georgina took a drink in an effort to warm the cold that had gripped her insides the minute she'd heard "his" voice on the phone.

"Are you sure you're okay?" Alex asked, his handsome features fraught with concern.

"I'm fine. It was just such a shock." She took another drink of her coffee, subconsciously noting that Alex had ordered her favorite. But even the comfort of the familiar drink couldn't chase away the horror that still held her in its grip.

"What did his voice sound like? Young? Old? Any accent that you could discern?" Alex asked. He leaned toward her, as if he wanted to wrap her in his arms, and for just a brief moment she wished he would.

She remembered far too well how it had felt to be cradled in Alex's arms…the sense of safety, of security she had found there.

Instead she stared down into her cup and then looked back at him. "It wasn't his real voice. He obviously was using some kind of voice-altering equipment. Still, I know it sounds crazy, but I feel like I've been touched by pure evil."

She straightened her shoulders and drew a deep, steadying breath. She couldn't allow herself to get spooked by a single phone call—Alex would pull her off the case if she appeared that weak.

"What did your caller identification show?" Alex asked. She was pleased his voice held no sympathy, no coddling tone.

"Unknown caller," she replied, also glad that her voice held no sense of the cold turmoil inside her. "He probably made the call from a throwaway phone. He's too smart to allow himself to be traced." She paused a moment. "If it really was him, then why me?"

"I don't know. Maybe because you're the only woman on the team?"

"How would he even know that I'm on the team? The article this morning didn't mention any names."

"I don't have any answers for you right now," Alex replied, his voice deep and his eyes fierce as he held her gaze. "But I promise you that by tomorrow we'll have some. If there's a leak in the department, I'll get to the bottom of it."

She saw the depth of anger simmering in his beautiful eyes and would hate to be the person on the receiving end of that ire.

"We can't know for sure that it was really the perp who made the call," he said thoughtfully. He took a drink of his coffee and set the cup back down. "There were plenty of news reports out of Bachelor Moon when Sam and his wife and little Macy went missing. The call could have just come from some creep."

"Creeps don't generally know my phone number," she replied dryly.

"We'll figure it all out," he said in an obvious effort to soothe, but she knew it was more likely than not that they wouldn't learn how he had gotten her phone number.

They fell silent for the next few minutes. She sipped her drink while Alex slugged down his coffee and got up to order himself another one. She had a feeling it would be a sleepless night for him as well as for her.

Macy. Why had the caller mentioned the little girl who had already found purchase in Georgina's heart? Perhaps he had just reasoned that since she was a woman, the child would be the best way to get to her. What a calculating creep.

By the time Alex returned to the table, Michelle and the man who had stood behind her at the autographing table walked through the door.

The big bruiser had his arm around Michelle and a scowl on his face that indicated he was definitely not pleased to be here. "Why would the FBI want to talk to Michelle?" he asked as the two of them reached the table where Georgina and Alex were seated.

"Maybe you're the one we need to talk to," Alex countered as he stood.

Georgina released a sigh. She'd already had enough drama for one night. She didn't need a macho showdown between the two men. "Why don't we all sit down and we'll explain exactly what brought Michelle to our attention."

Michelle took the stool next to Georgina. "I already know why you want to talk to me. This overly protective brute is my boyfriend, Jax White. Sit down, Jax, and let them ask their questions."

Jax took a seat as Alex returned to his. "I know the people I wrote about in my book are missing," Michelle said. "But that's all I know about the situation."

"So the kidnapping of these agents isn't part of a publicity stunt to sell more books?" Alex asked.

Michelle shot him a derisive look. "I don't subscribe to the 'Any publicity is good publicity' theory."

As Alex questioned Michelle further, Georgina tried to put the phone call out of her head and instead get a read on the woman and man seated at the table with them.

"I have some contacts in the agency," Michelle said, "and they pointed me to Sam Connelly, Amberly Caldwell and Jackson Revannaugh as three of the best profilers who had all recently solved fairly high-profile cases. I decided to showcase them in the book as some of the best of the best when it comes to catching killers."

"And exactly how did you do your research?" Georgina asked.

"She sure as hell didn't kidnap the agents," Jax exclaimed in obvious irritation.

Michelle ignored his outburst. "Unfortunately none of the agents would grant me interviews, so I did my research the hard way—by getting files on the cases they'd worked, by reading every article and news item I could find. I traveled to Mystic Lake and here to Baton Rouge to talk to some of the people who were involved with the crimes. I talked to the people in the towns, friends of the missing people. I also tried to talk to friends of the FBI agents. Unfortunately they all refused to talk to me."

Her chin rose defensively. "I worked hard to write

the stories of heroes and the criminals that they caught. I saw in the paper this morning that a task force had been formed to deal with the case of the missing FBI agents. I knew you'd be coming to question me, but I can't help you. I don't know what happened to them. I can't help you in any way in your investigation."

Jax stood and placed an arm around Michelle's shoulder. "Are we through here?"

"One more question…where were the two of you four nights ago?" Alex asked.

"At my home in New Orleans," Michelle answered without hesitation. She exchanged a glance with Jax.

"Do the two of you live together?" Georgina asked.

Michelle hesitated a beat before replying. "No, but Jax spends most nights at my place. I'm sure he was with me four nights ago."

Jax squeezed her shoulder. "And now I think we're through here." Michelle rose as if his hand on her shoulder was a magical wand that lifted her off the stool.

"Where can we reach you if we need to ask you more questions?" Alex asked.

"I'm leaving tomorrow on a book tour. If you'll give me your email or fax number I'll have my agent send you my itinerary," Michelle said.

Alex pulled a card from his pocket. "My cell phone and email is there. If I don't get that itinerary from your agent by noon tomorrow, then we're going to have problems."

Michelle nodded and the two of them left the coffee shop.

"Want another coffee?" Alex asked.

"No thanks. I think I'm ready to call it a day." She

knew they'd talk about this little interview in the car, but once the author and her boyfriend had disappeared from sight, the phone call Georgina had received filled her head once again.

Minutes later they were in Alex's car and headed toward her house. "I feel inclined to do a little background check on Mr. Jax White," Alex said.

"Probably wouldn't hurt," she agreed. "There was just a moment when Michelle said that Jax was with her on the night that Jackson and Marjorie disappeared that I didn't quite believe her."

"Maybe he decided to help his lover get a little extra publicity with her book," Alex said. "He's big enough to carry bodies over his shoulders and he looks like a man who might have a record."

"And he knew I was an FBI agent and had time before they met us here to make that phone call." Her stomach ached as she thought of the call.

They spoke no more until he pulled into her driveway. He cut the engine, turned out the car lights and then looked at her, his features visible in the streetlight next to her driveway.

"You want me to take your cell phone?" he asked.

She frowned at him in surprise. "Why would I want you to do that?"

"In case he calls again…so you don't have to deal with it."

"If he calls again it's because for some reason he wants to talk to me. You can't protect me, Alex. I can handle this. I'm fine."

She saw the frown that shot across his brow. "You're

always so damn strong, Georgina. You never need anyone."

She drew in a breath. "Are we talking about a phone call or are we discussing personal history?"

Leaning his head back, he raked a hand through his thick dark hair. "I don't know, maybe a little of both," he admitted.

"I won't discuss history," she replied. "What's done is done. All I'm interested in is catching this guy and saving not only our fellow agents but precious little Macy. I'll keep my phone and if he calls again I'll record the call and you'll be the first to know."

She opened the car door in an effort to stanch any further conversation that might turn to old heartaches and failures. "I can do my job, Alex. I don't need you to do anything but watch my back as a good partner would."

She got out of the car and shut the door and hurried toward her house. It was only when she was inside that she saw the lights on Alex's car beam on and then he pulled out of the driveway.

She locked her door and then went into her living room where she placed her gun, her official identification and her cell phone on the coffee table. She didn't want to admit that the phone call had completely creeped her out. The fact that the person on the other end of the line had called her by name had ignited a fear in her that she hadn't felt for a very long time.

Had the call really come from the man who held little Macy and the others captive? And why had he focused his attention on her when there were seven other members of the task force?

Maybe it was just some jerk who had managed to get her phone number and make the call. Crimes often brought out the mentally ill and the pranksters to play in the game.

Still, she couldn't discount the sharp intuition that told her he'd been the real deal.

She got up from the sofa and moved to the window to peer outside into the night. Her front yard held trees and bushes, hiding places for somebody who might be watching her.

Was he out there right now?

Watching her?

For the first time since her divorce she wished Alex were here with her, to assure her that the boogeyman wasn't after her, to hold her in his big strong arms and make her feel safe.

She'd told him she was fine, that she didn't need anyone. The truth was she was afraid to tap into any need she might possess.

Needing anyone, loving anyone made you vulnerable, made you appear weak. And Georgina knew better than anyone that weakness could set the predators circling overhead. And they would circle until you were too weak to fight them off when they attacked.

ALEXANDER DROVE AIMLESSLY after leaving Georgina's house. He often did his best thinking while in a car cruising without any specific direction, and at this moment he had a lot on his mind.

He wasn't particularly satisfied that Michelle and Jax hadn't pulled off a world-class publicity stunt. The two had set off tiny alarm bells in his head, but it was too early for the alarms to be a signal that they were guilty.

It would be interesting to see how this case played out as Michelle went on her book tour, if the kidnappings became a tool for garnering her publicity.

His bigger concern was the call Georgina had received, a call she was certain was from the man they hunted. He'd expected the perp to make contact again, but he'd assumed it would be by another note sent to headquarters. He hadn't expected the "reach out and touch someone" approach.

He definitely hadn't expected Georgina to be the one touched so personally by the perp. If it had really been him...if it hadn't been some kind of sick prank phone call, he reminded himself.

He knew he'd gone against protocol by not taking her phone away from her and carrying it immediately to one of the tech men to see if they could identify the location from where the call had come.

Turning down a dark side street, he knew he was betting on three things...that the call had probably come from a phone they wouldn't be able to trace, that the call itself hadn't lasted long enough for any kind of a trace, and finally that the potential perp would call her again.

Tightening his fingers on the steering wheel, he thought of that instant when he'd seen fear in the depths of her beautiful green eyes, when he'd seen the faint tremor of her hand as she'd placed her cell phone on the table. She'd recovered quickly, as she always did... as she always had.

As much as he'd loved her, that was the part of her that had frustrated him to distraction during their marriage. She gave him all the passion she had in her heart, in her soul, when they made love, but she never gave him her hopes, her fears or her dreams.

She'd given freely of her body, but had offered him no intimacy of her heart or soul, had shared nothing of her past to allow him to see what kind of influences had made her into the woman she'd become.

As he turned the car to head home, he told himself the last thing he should be doing was thinking about the days and nights he'd spent with Georgina, the love for her that still simmered in the very depths of his heart despite the fact that she'd walked away from their marriage seemingly without a backward glance.

He had a case to solve, seven people who were depending on him to find them. What he'd like to know was how the perp had focused in on Georgina? Had he read the paper that morning and managed to dig up the names of the people on the task force? Had he zeroed in on Georgina because she was the only woman on the team?

There was no doubt that there was a snitch someplace in the office. There was always a snitch willing to sell out names of agents and/or details of ongoing cases. There was always a bad apple somewhere. Alexander just wished he could be certain that the bad apple wasn't on his task force.

He would watch them all closely, and if he discovered that one of his men had given up Georgina's name to a reporter or anyone else, he'd see that the man no longer had a job, and no longer had a full set of teeth.

Pulling into the driveway of the house he'd once shared with Georgina, a deep weariness tugged at him.

He'd barely slept the night before and hoped tonight he would sleep without dreams.

He needed to be fresh and alert to begin a new day. He parked and got out of the car and entered the house that hadn't felt like home since the day Georgina had left.

Minutes later he stood in the master bath shower, allowing hot pellets of water to pummel his body. Once the tension of the day had eased away, he shut off the water and stepped out of the stall.

A large towel awaited him, along with a clean pair of boxers that served as his nightwear. He wasn't going to spend a single minute looking at files tonight. He just wanted to get into bed and sleep without dreams until dawn.

The bed seemed to embrace him as he fell supine and pulled the sheet up around his shoulders. He forced himself to empty his mind as he stared up at the patterns the moon made on the ceiling as the faint lunar light drifted through his curtains.

He must have fallen asleep immediately for the nightmare unfolded in horrifying, familiar detail. He drove the car at breakneck speed, knowing the killer held Kelly Gilmer in the old warehouse on Walker Street.

The killer was on his phone talking to Alexander, taunting him, unaware that Alexander was closing in. Through the line in the background he could hear Kelly begging for her life.

"Just let her go," Alexander said. "Daniel, if you walk away now we can work things out."

"I've killed three other women. How you going to work that out?" Daniel had screamed. "She's a faithless slut, just like the others before her and she deserves to die."

Alexander pulled to a halt in front of the warehouse, his heart beating so fast he feared he'd drop dead before he got inside where Kelly needed a hero. He desperately needed to be that hero.

He left the phone in the car with Daniel ranting and raving and stealthily made his way to the warehouse door. He opened it, his gun leading the way, as he slid through and looked around the dim building to get his bearings.

Daniel and Kelly's voices came from a room just ahead. Alexander crept forward, energized by the fact that Kelly was still well enough to plead for her life.

He stepped into the room, and instantly saw Daniel straddling Kelly, a wicked big knife in his hands. "Freeze!" Alexander screamed.

Daniel Bowie, a man who had kept the FBI busy by killing three other women, smiled at Alexander and then plunged the knife downward. Alexander fired his gun, shooting the young man in his chest.

As Daniel crumpled over, Alexander rushed to Kelly, already knowing it was too late, that she was dead. As he reached her, he looked down and instead of seeing Kelly's unseeing blue eyes, it was Georgina staring up at him with sightless green eyes.

He awoke, heart pounding and automatically reached to the other side of the bed. In his sleep-groggy mind, with the horror of the dream playing inside his head, it was only when he touched the cold empty sheets next to him that he remembered Georgina wasn't there. She hadn't been there for a very long time.

Dawn light crept through the windows and the sound of birds beginning to sing their morning songs pulled him out of bed. The dream was a familiar one since Kelly Gilmer's death, although Georgina had never made an appearance in his nightscape before now.

By the time he was dressed and drinking a cup of coffee in the large airy kitchen, he knew that the phone call she'd received bothered him more than he realized.

Although she was a seasoned agent and well trained in self-defense, fear for her knotted in the pit of his stomach. She would hate him for being afraid for her. She would hate him feeling anything for her.

But he couldn't help it. He felt as if she'd been personally touched by a malevolent force and he could only pray that the man who had called her had either been a fake or had no plans to touch her again.

Chapter Five

It had been a quiet day, with agents drifting in and out of the war room and everyone busy with their own particular task. First thing that morning Alex had asked Georgina to dig up everything she could on Michelle Davison and her boyfriend, Jax.

Since it was Sunday, Alex had given Nicholas, Matt and Jeff the day off. The rest of the team continued to work as if it were any other day of the week.

Georgina had spent the morning gathering information from traditional sources, checking out police records, news articles and whatever else she could find. Her cell phone sat on the table in front of her. Thankfully it had remained silent.

After a quick lunch, Alexander had left to go speak to the director, and Tim had gone on some mission of his own, leaving his partner, Jeff, to keep working on potential locations.

Georgina had finally moved on to social media sites, her eyes starting to glaze over as she read posts and looked at photos.

"I can't believe what people post on these public sites," she said as she found a photo of Jax half-naked and with a half-crazy look in his eyes. The caption read: The Exterminator, Got a Problem? I Can Handle It. And then it went on to say that he was a professional bodyguard/bouncer.

Frank, who was seated next to her, leaned over and looked at her computer screen, then shook his head. "I keep telling my daughters that what they put out there is out there forever," he said. "But in a house full of females, my voice is rarely heard," he said jokingly.

Georgina smiled. Frank not only had a beautiful, strong wife, but he also had four girls between the ages of eleven and seventeen. Her smile faded, she looked pointedly at Nicholas's empty chair and leaned closer so that only Frank would hear her. "It seems like your partner isn't listening to your voice very well, either."

Frank gave her a look of disgust. "He's a showboat. I keep telling myself he's young and trying to make his mark, but a task force isn't the time or place to play by your own rules. I'm glad he's off today. It's bad enough I'll have to deal with him again tomorrow."

He kept his voice low as well and Georgina knew he would say nothing to anyone else. As a team player, Frank wouldn't want to bring dissension among the group.

As Frank got back to work, Georgina rubbed her eyes and got up to get herself a cup of coffee. All the members of the task force had been told about the phone call she'd received the night before.

Tim was at this moment working with her cell phone company in an effort to get the record of the call, and then triangulate pings off cell phone towers to get a location from where the call had come. He would also work with them in an effort to identify the specific phone number of the caller and then would begin to search for serial numbers and stores where the phone might have been bought.

She didn't expect him to have any real information for a week or two. He might know a general area where the call had come from any time, but it would take much longer to learn more facts about the phone used to make the call to her.

With her coffee cup in hand, she returned to her seat at the table. She knew when Alex returned to the room he'd expect updates from the agents working.

She had a ton of information about Michelle Davison and her brute boyfriend. What she didn't have was any evidence that might point to them as persons of interest other than the book Michelle had written.

Tim had returned to the room and he and Terry had their heads together working off a single computer screen that had Google Earth up to focus on the Baton Rouge area.

They were all looking for a needle in a haystack… a location where seven people could be held, a man or men who had managed to kidnap those people without being seen, without leaving behind a single clue.

She stared at her phone, almost willing it to ring, almost wanting to get another call. While the idea of having any kind of personal interaction with a self-pronounced potential serial killer chilled her, she also knew that if he connected with her, he might make a mistake.

He could unconsciously give her a piece of information that might make it easier to identify him. There might be background noises on the call that could be magnified by tech workers to focus a search on a particular area of town.

She'd just gotten back to work when Alex came into the room. She glanced at her watch, surprised to realize it was after four. Surfing the internet had made the hours of the day melt away.

"I don't sense much excitement in here," he said as he went to the head of the table.

Frank shrugged. "Not much exciting to relate.

"I just finished speaking to Director Miller and Lieutenant Craig Burnett from the police department. He's agreed to have ten officers be our feet on the ground in checking out abandoned warehouses and factories and whatever building might be a potential hiding place for a kidnapper with seven hostages."

Alex turned to look at the two agents at the opposite end of the table from Georgina. "Any addresses you two get together on a list, give them to Lieutenant Burnett. He'll be checking in here every morning and working as a liaison between us and the police."

He moved his gaze to Frank. "I want you to get photos of all the victims made into posters and distributed all around town."

"We're officially taking this public?" Frank asked.

Alex nodded. "Miller is holding a news conference first thing in the morning. We're all to be press-ready by nine. We're setting up a TIPS line and hoping that by blanketing the city with posters, somebody saw something that might break the investigation wide open."

He turned to face Georgina and at that moment her cell phone rang. She immediately knew it was *him*. She didn't need to see the unknown number that her caller identification displayed.

The war room was completely silent and all the men stared at her as she picked up the phone and hit Speaker and Record as she answered. "Agent Beaumont," she said, aware of Alex moving closer.

"Such formality. May I call you Georgina?" It was the same deep voice, obviously computer-altered. "I thought we were going to be friends."

"You can call me Georgina." Her mouth was achingly dry. "And what should I call you?"

Before there could be a reply Alex grabbed the phone from her. "This is Special Agent Alexander Harkins. I'm the lead investigator on this case. I think I'm the one you want to talk to."

"If I'd wanted to talk to you, I would have called your phone, Agent Alexander Harkins." There was an audible click, letting everyone in the room know that the caller had hung up.

Georgina snatched her phone away from Alex, angry that he'd interfered and screwed up what might have been a call that contained a clue, concerned that he'd done so in an effort to protect her.

Before she could voice her outrage over his action, her phone rang again. She glared at Alex, daring him to pull another stunt, and then once again hit Speaker and Record and answered the call.

"Don't let that happen again." It was obvious the man on the phone had been angered.

"It won't," Georgina replied with another glare at Alex. Even though her heart was beating way too fast, despite the fact that the cold chill of evil had crept from the cell phone to take over every part of her body, she knew this connection was their best chance to catch the man.

"You never told me what I should call you," she said.

"FBI-trained serial killer is a mouthful, isn't it? Why don't you call me Bob?"

"Okay, Bob." It didn't seem right that evil should go by the name of Bob, but she was playing his game. "Is there a reason you want to talk to me, Bob?" She kept her gaze focused on the phone that was on the table in front of her and refused to look at any of the men in the room.

"I know you and your team are working very hard to try to find me, but in the meantime I've done a little research of my own…some research on you."

Georgina couldn't imagine that her blood could get any colder, but his words shot a new icy chill through her veins. "You must have been bored to death," she replied, glad that her voice didn't betray any of the emotions roaring through her.

"On the contrary, I think you and I have a lot of things in common."

Revulsion rose at his words. She couldn't imagine what she could possibly have in common with this man. "How do I know that you're really the person who kidnapped the FBI agents and their loved ones?" she asked, deciding to ignore his previous words.

"If you'd like me to I could send you Sam Connelly's ear in the mail. Or perhaps you would prefer a finger from Amberly Caldwell."

Georgina flinched. "That isn't necessary. Just let me speak to one of them."

"I might be able to arrange that, but first I want to talk to you about your childhood."

Georgina's throat closed off as a flash of old memories torched through her brain. She was grateful the phone was on the table for she would have probably dropped it as her hands began to tremble uncontrollably.

She quickly clenched them together and moved them to her lap beneath the table where nobody would be able to see them. "What about my childhood?"

"Was it good or bad?"

She thought about lying, she considered not allowing him to get any real piece of her, but she was also afraid that if he already knew the answer and she lied, she'd break trust with him and he'd stop calling and this chance for clues would be lost forever.

She was more than aware that building trust with him through the phone calls might be the only way they'd get any clues as to his identity. She desperately needed to build some mutual trust with him.

"It was bad," she finally replied. She looked up and found herself staring into the blue depths of Alex's eyes. How many times had he asked her about her childhood and she'd always deflected the conversation, had refused to give him any hint of the hell she'd endured.

It was a time of her life she refused to revisit except in the form of torturous nightmares and she would do it only now to hopefully save the lives of the people he held captive.

"Your mother and father, did you ever dream of killing them?"

"I already answered one of your questions. Now you need to let me talk to one of your captives before I answer any more." She broke eye contact with Alex and held her breath, hoping for honor from a creep.

"Who do you want to hear from?"

"Jackson," Alex whispered.

"Macy," Georgina replied.

There was a long moment of silence. Georgina held her breath, knowing it was possible she would face Alex's wrath once the call eventually ended.

"Hello?"

The childish voice squeezed Georgina's heart painfully tight. "Macy? My name is Georgina."

"Are you going to come and get us?"

"Who is with you?"

"There's Daddy Sam and my mom and Ms. Amberly and Mr. Caldwell and Mr. Revannaugh and Ms. Clinton. We're all waiting for you to come and find us. We all just want to go home." A small sob choked from her.

"Where are you, honey?"

"We're in cages," she replied.

Georgina frowned. "Cages?"

"You talked to the little girl, now it's my turn again," Bob said. "Now, answer my question. Did you ever dream of killing your mother and father?"

"Never," she replied and then couldn't help but add, "I sometimes wished them dead, but I never entertained the idea of actually killing them myself."

Pressure filled her chest, making it difficult for her to breathe as emotions untapped for nearly a lifetime rushed in. She hated Bob for making her remember, for making her feel those emotions she'd tried so hard to put behind her.

"For years I dreamed of killing my mother and father, and then one day when I was twenty-five years old, I went back to the old homestead and I did it. I killed them. They were my first victims," he said. The line went dead.

THE SILENCE IN the room was deafening. Thoughts thundered through Alexander's head as he stared at the woman he'd once been married to, a woman who had just given more information about her past to a killer than she'd ever shared with him.

She raised her head to meet his gaze, her green eyes hard and impossible to read. "I'm sorry. I probably should have asked to speak to one of the men, but in my mind Macy was…is the most expendable and I needed to make sure she was still alive."

"It's fine," Alexander replied. He tried to ignore the paleness of her cheeks, the obvious toll the phone call had taken on her.

"So, if Bob is to be believed, he murdered his parents," Frank said. "Even though he'd altered his voice, he didn't sound that old…maybe early- to mid-thirties."

"Then the murder of his parents would have happened within the past ten years or so," Terry said.

"And if he killed his parents, then why isn't he in prison?" Tim asked.

Alexander's attention was split between the conversation going on among the team and Georgina, who seemed to have disappeared into herself. Her shoulders were slumped and her gaze remained focused on the cell phone on the table in front of her.

He told himself it wasn't just because he'd been her husband and that it wasn't because on some deep level he still loved her that he was concerned. He would be concerned about any of the team members who had shared a rather intimate conversation with a self-professed killer.

Tim took her phone and downloaded the message into his computer. As a techie, he could work on the recording to see if there were any background noises that could be amplified. He'd also try to chase down the number the call had come from.

Georgina remained quiet until they called it a day. As the men left the room, Alexander caught hold of her arm so he could talk to her alone.

"Are you all right?" he asked softly.

"I'm fine." Her shoulders stiffened in a familiar posture of defensiveness. Her eyes were a dark green that he'd never seen before, filled with shadows he could never breach, he would never fully understand.

"Want to grab coffee at Cup of Joe's before heading home?" He kept his tone light, knowing that if she sensed any concern for her in his voice she'd decline.

"Okay," she surprised him by saying.

Together they left the room and headed to the elevator. "At least we got a little more information," she said as they rode down to the first floor. "We know that right now they are all alive."

"And I'm adding to Terry and Matt's workload by having them check every case of any couple murdered in their homes or under suspicious circumstances in the past fifteen years in the state," he replied.

"That could take months of work," she said as they left the elevator and headed for the front door of the building.

Cup of Joe's was a small hole-in-the-wall coffee shop three buildings down from the FBI building. It was a popular place for tired agents to fuel up or wind down.

Joe's menu offered no fancy froufrou drinks, nothing but coffee and a variety of muffins, cookies and little cakes. As Georgina took a seat at one of the narrow booths against the wall, Alexander ordered two cups of coffee, one black and one with cream and sugar.

When he joined her with the drinks, she was curled into the corner between the back of the booth and the wall. She looked more fragile than he'd ever seen her. As he sat down, she quickly straightened, her eyes overly bright as if she were working too hard to keep it together.

He slid her coffee halfway across the table, but when she went to reach for it, he grabbed her hand in his. He held tight even as she tried to pull away.

"Just sit for a minute and let me hold your hand," he said softly.

"I don't need hand-holding," she protested, but she didn't attempt to pull her hand away again.

"You were amazing," he said. "You kept your cool and played your own game with him. You forced him into letting us hear from one of the victims."

"It didn't feel amazing. It was terrifying," she admitted. "I was so afraid that if I said something wrong there would be terrible consequences."

This time when she pulled her hand back, he released it and watched as she wrapped both her slightly trembling hands around the hot foam cup of coffee.

Alexander picked up his own cup and leaned back against the booth. "For some reason or another it's obvious that he's decided he wants a relationship with you."

Her eyes widened but quickly resumed their normal shape. "If that's what it takes to solve this, then I'll be his best phone buddy."

Protests rose to his throat, but he swallowed them. The need to protect her from having any contact with this man was overwhelming, but he had to think of what was in the best interest of solving the crime. She was a member of the task force. It was her job to do whatever she could to help catch the creep.

He couldn't think like a man who needed to protect his woman. She hadn't been his woman in a very long time. When he looked back on their marriage, he sometimes wondered if she'd ever really been his woman.

They sat in silence, sipping their hot coffee. The silence wasn't uncomfortable. He was accustomed to her being a woman of few words.

It was finally she who broke the silence. "If what he said about his parents is true, then he's already killed and won't hesitate to kill again." She took another sip of her drink and then continued. "You know he won't let them live. Once he's gotten whatever he thinks he needs from them, he'll kill them all."

Her eyes held a hollowness, as if she were already grieving for their loss. He didn't try to tell her differently. He knew what she said was true. "All the more reason we've got to work every angle to find him before that can happen."

"He'll keep calling me." She said it as a statement, not as a question.

Alexander nodded. "Yes, I think he will. He's connected with you and I think he'll want to maintain that connection until the end, whatever the end looks like." He took another drink of his coffee and then leaned forward. "What you said, about your childhood being bad. Was that true?"

She released a sigh, as if she'd known he'd ask and yet had hoped he wouldn't. "Yes, it's true, I had a difficult childhood, but it's not something I want to talk about." Her chin lifted a bit, as if daring him to pursue the topic.

It had always been that way with her. When he'd attempted to dig too deep, he'd been met with resistance. He'd quickly learned not to try to get into anything about her past. He'd just been happy to have her in his life. But apparently he hadn't been enough for her.

"Maybe the tech department and Tim will be able to enhance any background noise on the recording or they'll be able to get a handle on his speech pattern and give us some ideas about education or where he might be from if he isn't a native," he said.

"Hopefully, when he calls again, I'll be able to get more from him. More about the murder of his parents, more of his background information or something else important," she said. "We need to find them." Her eyes took on a haunted look. "Macy will be the first one he'll kill. Even though she's with her mother and father, she has to be so afraid. No child should ever be that afraid."

He had to fight his instinct to once again reach out and grab her hand, to get up and move to sit beside her and pull her into his arms. He had a feeling she knew that kind of fear, the kind no child should ever know. She had lived it in her "bad" childhood.

"You know how dangerous it is for you to lose your objectivity," he said softly. "You know that it's not good to identify too closely with any victim or the perp. Trust me, I lived it. Get too emotionally involved with a victim and it will destroy you if things go bad."

She took a drink of her coffee, her gaze locked with his. "Do you still have nightmares?"

"Only when I sleep," he said in an effort to lighten the mood. "What about you?"

"Occasionally I have bad dreams, but not as often as I used to. I work so hard I usually fall into bed too exhausted to dream."

"That's good, and I hope it stays that way."

She smiled at him. "Was this a mental-wellness-check cup of coffee?"

He returned her smile. "Maybe a little bit. It would shake up any seasoned agent to be receiving phone calls from a perp. I should have known you'd be strong enough to handle it."

"If it's a chance to get those people home safely, then I can handle anything." She finished her coffee and grabbed her purse. "I need to get home."

"Wait a minute. I'll walk you to your car since we're parked in the same lot." He got up and threw their disposable coffee cups into a trash bin and then they stepped out into the September night air.

"It's odd, he called me both times at about the same time of the day," she said as they headed back down the sidewalk toward the parking lot behind the FBI building. "Around four o'clock."

"Maybe he works a job and that's his break time?" Alexander speculated.

"It's Sunday, you would think he wouldn't be at work at all today."

"We'll have to wait and see if the pattern continues. That could be another potential clue in this mess we have."

"Terry and Matt said the investigations that took place in Bachelor Moon and in Mystic Lake look pretty solid, so they probably aren't going to find anything there to help us."

"How about we end the night by not talking about the crimes," he said.

She cast him a sideways glance. "Then what do you want to talk about?"

"I don't know…the weather, the latest movie you've seen, what you're reading?"

She grinned at him, that impish grin that always managed to stir a wealth of emotion inside him. "The weather is sultry, I can't remember the last movie I saw and I'm reading Michelle Davison's book."

"And that begs the questions that lead right back to talking about the case," he replied with an answering grin. "So, learning anything new about the missing agents?"

"Actually, I didn't know that Jackson's father was a criminal," she replied.

A shaft of pain shot through him at thoughts of his friend. "It was Jackson's biggest shame. His father was a con man who married wealthy older women and then drained their savings and divorced them or arranged for accidents to happen to them. Jackson helped put his father in prison, but when he got out, he wanted Jackson to pay. When Jackson was in Kansas City, he had a showdown with his father, who was shot to death by another agent."

"That part of it wasn't in the book," she said as they reached her car.

"It only happened a couple of days before Jackson came back here. Michelle wouldn't have known about it when she wrote the book. She was focused solely on Jackson's role in the Twilight Killer case."

"Well, I guess I'll see you at seven in the morning," she said as she clicked her key fob to unlock her doors.

He grabbed her arm and turned her back to face him before she could open her car door. She looked up at him curiously. "Georgina, I just want to warn you not to let him get inside your head."

Unable to help himself, he reached up and stroked two fingers down her delicate jawline, stopping when he reached her chin. It was an old habit, one that had always ended before with him tipping her head back so he could take total possession of her lips.

He wanted to kiss her, he desperately wanted to wrap his arms around her and kiss her until her head spun and her brain was filled with nothing but him.

To his surprise, without him urging her chin upward, she dropped her head back slightly, as if inviting him to finish the old routine.

He didn't hesitate. He lowered his mouth to hers, tentatively at first and when she didn't protest he wrapped his arms around her, pulled her close and deepened the kiss.

She tasted like coffee and heat. The kiss evoked old memories. She tasted like home. He wanted to kiss her forever, but before he could make a fool of himself, he reluctantly ended the kiss and released her from his arms.

She stared at him for a long moment and raised a finger to rub across her full lower lip. "You know we can't go back, Alex," she said softly.

"I know," he replied. "But if that creep starts to mess with your mind, if he gets too far into your head, I want you to think about me, about kissing me and hopefully that will keep you grounded."

"You have a lot of confidence in the power of your kiss," she said with a wry smile.

He laughed. "You used to tell me that when I kissed you, you couldn't think about anything else. Maybe some of that old magic still exists…at least enough to keep you mentally stable against a killer."

"We'll see," she replied and then got into her car. With a wave of her hand, she started the engine and pulled out.

He watched her taillights until they disappeared from view and only then did he walk to his own car. He sat behind the steering wheel and leaned his head back.

The truth was that he wanted to go back in time. He wanted a do-over with Georgina. He'd never understood why she'd walked out on him in the first place.

She'd been by his side when he'd gone through the worst of his depression, and when things seemed to finally be back on track, when he'd eventually gotten his head back on straight, she'd decided she needed out and he had been left with questions that had never been answered.

He hoped by the time they solved this crime he'd have some of those questions answered and maybe, just maybe, he and Georgina would be back together where he believed they belonged.

Chapter Six

That kiss.

That damnable kiss.

It had kept her tossing and turning all night, fighting against the old feelings the kiss had evoked. When she'd finally fallen asleep, she had dreamed of the two of them together in the bed in their master suite making love.

Alex had been a passionate man and he'd stirred a want, a desire inside her she'd never known before him. He was like an intoxicant to her and she to him. She'd wanted him the first time she'd met him and she'd wanted him the day she walked away from him.

The kiss and the memories of those dreams had remained in her head the next day when she arrived at work. She'd timed her arrival to be right at seven, knowing that most of the team would already be present and there would be no time for any personal talk between her and Alex.

She had to keep things strictly professional between them, and last night she'd allowed a slip that couldn't be repeated. She couldn't be pulled back into Alex's life in any meaningful way. He deserved a better woman than she would ever be.

"Let's get updates," Alex said as Georgina slid into her chair at the conference table.

"Georgina, you've been researching Michelle Davison and Jax White. Anything earth-shattering come from your work so far?"

"Michelle was born and raised here in Baton Rouge. She attended the Baton Rouge College, and soon after graduating with a degree in journalism, she published her first book, an in-depth look at the Baxter kidnapping case. For those of you who don't know, Kimberly Baxter was kidnapped at the age of sixteen and held captive for two years at which time she managed to escape. The book got rave reviews and Michelle has written three more books since then, the latest the one that brought her to our attention."

Part of her information she'd gained the day before, but much of what she had learned had occurred last night when Alex's kiss had burned her lips and made sleep impossible.

"She's never been arrested, hasn't even had a traffic ticket and seems to be squeaky clean," she continued. "But that's not the case with her boyfriend. Before he hooked up with Michelle three years ago, he was in and out of jail for assault, public drunkenness and a variety of misdemeanors. The most important point of interest I found out late last night is that Jax's parents died in a fire in their home nine years ago while Jax was away on a floating trip with some buddies. I'm waiting to get a file on the case to look further into their deaths."

"So the author and her boyfriend don't fall off our persons-of-interest list," Frank said.

Alex turned to the whiteboard where both Michelle's

and Jax's names were written in bold red marker. "They'll stay right there until we can clear them of any culpability."

"Too bad they're up there all alone," Terry said.

"I might be able to add a name to that short list," Frank said. "I was surfing the internet late last night and discovered some kook who runs his own 'news' show. His name is Roger Cambridge and he's been following these cases since the family disappeared from Bachelor Moon. Last night he talked about the task force. He had all of our names listed and when I checked his previous posts, he had photos taken in Bachelor Moon and Mystic Lake during the investigations."

Georgina saw the light that shone from Alex's eyes, the shine of a predator scenting prey. She'd seen that same light in his eyes just before he'd taken her to bed. "Did you get an address?"

Frank nodded. "He lives in unit 215 at the Beacon Apartments just off Beacon Street, across from the college campus. He's twenty-eight years old, and according to the stats I checked he has a growing fan base. He does his news show three times a week, on Sunday, Tuesday and Thursday nights."

Georgina knew the apartment complex. It catered to college students who preferred parties to class work, and she knew that the local cops were regulars there on the weekends, busting up fights or arresting underage drinkers.

"We've handed addresses of over forty empty buildings that are surrounded by more than three acres of land to the cops," Tim said. "They're in the process of checking out those locations while Jeff and I continue to compile addresses."

Alex nodded and then turned his gaze to Nicholas, who had looked surprised by Frank's new information. "Looks like your partner just evened the score for your showboating yesterday," he said. "Both of you continue to work together to get me more connections, no matter how tenuous between these people." He directed his gaze at Nicholas. "Team players, that's what I want from everyone."

Nicholas gave a curt nod of his head, but Georgina had a feeling this little dressing down wouldn't affect the eager agent's desire to lone-wolf it and save the day.

"You all have your work," Alex continued. "Georgina and I are taking off to check out Roger Cambridge. If anything breaks here, call me."

Georgina stood as Alex left the head of the table. Despite the fact that it was obvious they would once again be spending time alone, she was determined that their conversation would remain strictly professional.

He was worried about their killer getting into her head, but she was equally concerned about Alex getting into her head. She couldn't allow either man in.

"Sleep well?" he asked as they exited the building and headed toward his car.

"Like a baby," she replied. Was he wondering if the kiss had shaken her up? Was he hoping that it had disturbed her, forced her to remember how it had once been between them?

The physical side of their marriage had never been at issue. They had both been passionate and giving and each time they'd made love it had been beyond magical.

"How did you sleep?" she asked and then instantly regretted the question as his eyes deepened and a familiar slow grin curled his lips.

"Do you want me to tell you about my dreams?" he asked.

"Not unless you thought of something to help solve the case," she replied. She opened the passenger door and got into the car, wondering if he'd had the same kind of erotic dreams she'd had of them together.

Damn that kiss anyway.

"Thank God I talked Miller into doing the press interview this morning without our attendance," he said as he made the turn to take them toward the college campus.

"I always hate being in a press conference," she replied. "We all stand behind Miller looking like trained monkeys ready for action."

Alexander laughed. "I never really thought about it that way before." They were silent for a few miles and then he spoke again, knowing he was navigating dangerous topics.

"Do you ever think about it? About our marriage? About our time together?" he asked.

"Sometimes," she admitted after a long hesitation.

"We had some good times." He shot her a surreptitious glance. She remained staring straight ahead out the window and she was just as beautiful in profile as she was straight-on.

"We did," she agreed, not looking at him. "But that was then and this is now. Every time we're alone together, you can't talk about the past. It's over, Alex, and we're here to do a job."

She didn't turn to look at him and for that reason an edge of frustration rippled through him. "I was happy with you." He pulled into a parking spot in front of the Beacon Apartments. He cut the engine but remained buckled in the seat. He stared at her until she sighed and turned to look at him. "I just want to know what happened, what I did to make you leave. Was it because I fell apart after the Gilmer case?" He'd always wondered if the weakness he'd shown after that case had somehow turned her off, had made her see him as less of a man.

"Oh, Alex, no. It had nothing to do with you." Her eyes shimmered in the morning light, like green leaves on a newly budded tree. "I just wasn't happy. I realized that I wasn't meant to be in a relationship."

Her eyes darkened with an uncharacteristic plea. "You have to leave it alone. Please don't pick at old scabs. Otherwise I'll have to request that I be taken off the task force and that will hurt my career."

Alexander suddenly felt small, and recognized in some part of his brain that he was trying to force something from Georgina that she couldn't or wouldn't give to him. He had to let it go. He had to let her go and stay with the unanswered questions that would always plague him where she was concerned.

"I'm sorry. I've been completely unprofessional where you're concerned and it won't happen again," he said sincerely.

"I just need you to treat me as part of the team," she said. "Nothing more and nothing less."

"Done," he said and unbuckled his seat belt. "Now, let's go in and see what the deal is with this hotshot internet reporter."

He heard her sigh of relief as she got out of the passenger door and he mentally kicked himself for being a fool. He hadn't realized until now that he'd been holding onto the thought of them somehow, someway getting back together again since the moment she'd left him.

He had to keep his head in the game of this case. It was time to let go of foolish fantasies that would never be. Georgina was gone to him as the seven missing people were gone to the world. He would do everything in his power to find those seven people, but he had to let Georgina go.

Minutes later they stood in front of unit 215. The hallway stank of stale smoke and food, with an underlay of urine and vomit…definitely a party floor. The apartments were quiet. The students who lived here either were still sleeping or had already left for early morning classes.

As they approached unit 215, he couldn't help but notice that Georgina appeared more relaxed than she'd been since the first time she'd walked into the conference room that morning and saw him there.

He knocked on the door where Roger Cambridge resided. There was no reply. He knocked again, this time harder. "Hang on, wait a damn minute," a deep male voice called from inside.

The door finally opened to reveal a big guy clad in an undershirt and boxers. His hair was light brown and definitely sporting the bed-head look. "What the hell?" he demanded. "Everyone knows I work nights and sleep late in the mornings."

"Sorry to interrupt your beauty sleep," Georgina said and gazed pointedly at his hair. "It's obvious your hair hasn't had enough." She flipped out her identification as Alexander showed his.

"We have some questions to ask you," Alexander said. "You want to do it out in the hallway or are you going to invite us in?"

Roger raked a hand through his unruly hair and then opened his door. "Come on in. Do you mind if I at least pull some pants on?"

"Go ahead," Alexander said as they stepped into the small living room that had the feel of a very low budget television studio. Several computers sat on a desk, along with a couple of high-powered lights on stands. A large bulletin board appeared to serve as a backdrop and held a map of the United States, photos of the missing FBI agents and photos of the crime scenes.

Alexander exchanged a glance with Georgina, who shrugged and sat on a sofa shoved against one wall. *Freaky fan, or just a freak making news so he can report it?* Alexander wondered.

Roger returned to the room, now clad in a pair of worn jeans and with his hair damp and combed. "I assume you're here to ask me questions about my part in the missing FBI agents case," he said. He picked up his cell phone from the desk. "Mind if I videotape this interview?"

"The only person doing any kind of taping is going to be me," Alex replied and pulled a small tape recorder from his pocket.

"Put your phone down," Georgina said in a stern voice.

He placed his phone back on the desk and then slumped down into the desk chair. "I can tell by your tones that there's no good cop / bad cop thing that's going to happen. You're both bad cops, right?"

"You've been watching too much television," Alexander replied dryly. "We just want to ask you some questions…like how you have photos of crimes scenes that haven't been released to the public."

He was particularly interested in the picture that depicted Sam and Daniella's kitchen, with the milk and cookies on the table and a chair overturned. That was the only scene where it was obvious something wrong had happened.

"I follow crime for my show." Roger leaned forward, his round face animated. "The Roger Dodger Crime Scene Show. Have either of you ever caught it on the internet?" He gave them no time to reply. "Well, I guess one of you did. Otherwise, you wouldn't be here."

"Actually it was a colleague of ours who caught your show last night," Alexander said. "And I'd like to know how you got that photo of the Connellys' kitchen. It was obviously taken during the crime scene investigation."

Roger beamed proudly. "Unfortunately, I can't divulge my sources. It's one of those amendment rights. But I'm very good at my job, and my job is to get as close to the investigation as possible, to make my viewers feel as if they know everything that's happening with these cases."

"Why these particular cases?" Georgina asked. "There's all kind of crimes happening all around the country."

"When I first heard that a former FBI agent, his wife and their kid had disappeared from Bachelor Moon, it felt like a story that might be big, so I immediately headed down to Bachelor Moon and started doing newscasts about that case."

"And how did you hear about the Mystic Lake case?" Alexander asked, at the same time trying not to be distracted by the scent of Georgina so close to him.

"I check all the major news sources all the time. I caught wind of that one from a Kansas City source and left here by plane. I rented a car in Kansas City and then drove to Mystic Lake and started on-location podcasts."

For the next hour Alexander and Georgina grilled the baby-face Roger Dodger, who appeared open and eager to help them in any way possible. Unfortunately, nothing he had to offer was any help.

By the time they left his apartment Alexander's head was jumbled with thoughts. Neither of them spoke until they were back in his car.

"I've heard of perps insinuating themselves into some element of the investigation," he said thoughtfully. "I don't know if that's the case with Roger or not."

"He's physically fit enough to be able to move the bodies if they were unconscious," Georgina replied. "And he definitely simmered with excitement while he talked about the case."

"Yeah, simmered with a little too much excitement in my mind. Something about him left a bad taste in my mouth." He started the car and pulled out of the apartment parking lot.

"So, he goes up on our whiteboard and we do more digging into who he really is and what, exactly, he's up to," he added. What little background information they had gotten from Roger would have to be vetted.

"That still makes our person of interest list pathetically short," Georgina replied.

"We're only a couple of days into this, Georgina. It's going to take time."

"I know. I just hope…" her voice trailed off as she turned to look out the passenger window.

She didn't have to finish her sentence; he knew exactly what she was going to say. She just hoped the seven people they sought had enough time to be found alive.

JACKSON REVANNAUGH HAD BEEN ANGRY ever since he'd awakened on a top bunk in a jail-like cell with Marjorie unconscious on the bunk below him. The last thing he'd remembered before arriving in the cell was making love to Marjorie and then falling asleep.

He'd gone to bed wearing boxers and when he'd become conscious he'd found a pair of his jeans and a T-shirt in the cell. There had also been clothes for Marjorie, who had been taken from the bed in her nightgown.

It had been six days since then, and in those days Jackson had come to know the others who shared the same fate. On one hand he was relieved to know that they were all alive; on the other hand he knew they were all in big trouble.

The only ray of sunshine was little Macy, who sang songs and made up stories about princesses being rescued by handsome princes. The sound of her sweet little voice coming from the cell on the other side of Amberly and Cole's broke his heart. No kid should be here. Nobody living and breathing should be here. Hell, he didn't even know where *here* was.

He'd already learned the daily routine. The creep who had taken them showed up each morning wearing a ski mask and bearing breakfast sandwiches and cups of coffee or juice. The trays were slid through a slot, just as prisoners were served in jail cells.

There was rarely any lunch, and then dinner was served the same way. There was just enough food to keep them alive, but not quite enough to allow them to thrive.

When their captor delivered the food, he never spoke, although Jackson had learned from the others that he'd interrogated Sam, Amberly and Cole several times.

Jackson now sat on the lower bunk, Marjorie curled up against him. Guilt weighed heavily on him. She shouldn't have been here. He'd encouraged her to leave Kansas City and come to Baton Rouge to continue the relationship they'd formed while he was working the case of the missing Amberly and Cole.

If he hadn't encouraged her, if he'd just walked away from her, then she wouldn't be sitting in this hellhole with him. She'd be safe at home.

He tightened his arm around her and she raised her head and looked at him, love shining from her eyes and pulling a lump into his throat. "I'm so sorry, Maggie," he said softly. "I should have just walked away from you and left you in Kansas City."

"I didn't want to stay in Kansas City. I wanted to be with you," she replied, keeping her voice low so that the others couldn't hear their conversation.

"And now here you are," he replied with a trace of bitterness.

"In your arms, exactly where I want to be," she said. "Jackson, I love you, and no matter what happens here, I will always love you."

His heart filled with his love for her. "And I will always love you." He lowered his lips and gave her a gentle kiss and at that moment the far door in the distance swung open and their captor walked in.

He grabbed a folding chair and positioned it in front of Jackson and Marjorie's cell. "I think it's time we have a little chat, Agent Revannaugh." He sat down.

"I can't imagine what we'd have to chat about," Jackson returned, aware of the silence from the other two cells.

"On the contrary, you have a wealth of information I need."

Marjorie threw herself against the bars. "Why don't you take off that stupid ski mask and face us? Why don't you just go to hell?"

The captor pulled a gun from his pocket and pointed it at Marjorie. "Agent Revannaugh, I suggest you get control of your woman or I'll take care of her and you can spend the rest of your time here with her rotting corpse."

Jackson instantly grabbed Marjorie and threw her behind him. "She won't be a problem. What kind of information do you want from me?" His chest was tight, but it eased slightly as Marjorie curled up on the bottom bunk and the man shoved his gun into his waistband.

"When you were chasing the Twilight Killer, what kind of mistakes did he make that eventually led to his arrest? He killed five women with baseball bats before you finally caught him."

What the hell? Jackson thought. That particular case was a little over two years old, and for a two-month period the women in Baton Rouge had been afraid to leave their homes at the time between day and night.

"He got sloppy," Jackson finally answered. "They always get sloppy and make mistakes."

"Like what?" The captor leaned forward as if eager to hear any information Jackson could impart.

"In that particular case we found the bat he'd used on his last victim in a storm drain. He'd gotten careless and hadn't bothered to wear gloves. We got a couple of good prints off it and the man was already in the system because of an arrest for domestic abuse."

"In your personal experience what other mistakes do killers make to get caught?"

Jackson frowned. This was all so bizarre. Who was this man who'd managed to get seven people in his lair? And where was this place where he kept them?

The question-and-answer period lasted for about twenty minutes. The man was totally focused on how criminals got caught, on what mistakes they made.

Jackson didn't pretend not to cooperate. The price was too high if he didn't. Besides, most of the information he had to impart could be found by studying any criminology book or the dozens of tomes written on profiling.

With a glance at his watch and appearing to be satisfied with the conversation, the man got up. He folded his chair and carried it to the wall.

"You're a mean Mr. Poopy Head," Macy said.

It was as if time stood still. Everyone froze as Macy's words hung in the air. The man pointed his fingers like a gun at her.

"Bang," he said and then left by the door he'd entered.

Chapter Seven

The next couple of days went by in agonizing slow ticks of the hands on the clocks. Georgina's phone had remained silent, and that worried her. She had hoped that the perp would continue to call at regular intervals. She had hoped that somehow the calls would give up some clues as to the identity of the man they sought. Each morning when she arrived, she set the phone in front of her on the table, just in case a call came in.

She was also frustrated by Alex, who had done nothing at all but what she'd asked, treated her as part of the team and nothing more.

It was exactly what she'd wanted and yet now that he appeared distant and completely professional, she realized she missed the way he'd looked at her before, as if he'd never really stopped loving her. She missed the private conversations that had gone beyond the case, even though most of them had made her uncomfortable.

She glanced up from her laptop to see him at the end of the conference table, immersed in paperwork. As usual he wore black slacks, but today he'd paired them with an ice-blue shirt that made his eyes appear a glacier-blue. His dark hair was slightly rumpled, only adding to his overall hotness.

She focused back on her computer, wondering if there would ever come a time when she didn't find him attractive, when she didn't look at him and remember what it had felt like to be naked with him, to feel his warm flesh against her own?

The case, she told herself. *Work on the case and stop thinking about Alex.* She'd been tasked with finding out everything she could about the hotshot self-proclaimed newsman, Roger Cambridge.

All the members of the team were in the room except Nicholas, who had left earlier to get some lunch. A cloud of frustration hung heavy in the air. Everyone felt the lack of forward motion, the stagnant condition of the case, despite the short length of time they'd been working it.

The press conference had gone off, posters of Jackson and Marjorie had been plastered all around town and the TIPS lines that had been set up in another conference room, manned by trained volunteers, were receiving dozens of calls.

The volunteers would be able to determine if the calls were the usual crazies or something that needed to be checked out. So far the TIPS line had yielded nothing worthwhile.

It was just after two and Georgina was fighting against an afternoon drain in energy. She got up from her chair and walked over to the coffeemaker and poured herself a cup. Before carrying it back to her chair, she stretched and tried to shove away the weariness of inactivity.

She was halfway back to her chair with the coffee when her cell phone rang. The coffee sloshed over the rim as she hurried to her seat, conscious of everyone's gaze focused on her.

Her insides trembled as she placed her cup on the table and then answered the phone, as usual punching speaker and record at the same time. "Agent Beaumont," she said.

"Ah, Georgina, have you missed me?" Bob asked.

"Actually I have," she replied. "I thought maybe you didn't want to be my friend anymore."

"You're my closest friend, Georgina, and I want to continue the discussion we were having the other day about family."

Georgina closed her eyes, a familiar pressure of pain filling her chest as she thought about her family. "I'll tell you what, why don't you let Macy go? Just drop her off at some mall or in the middle of a park and drive away and then we'll talk about my family."

"Georgina, are you trying to call the shots here?" Bob laughed, the sound a sinister one that crawled up her spine. "How about we talk about you first and then I'll consider your request to release the little princess."

A reckless hope buoyed up inside her as she kept her focus on the face of the cell phone. "Ask your questions, Bob, and then we'll see if you're a man of your word when it comes to reciprocating."

She felt Alex's presence right behind her, smelled the familiar scent of his cologne and a sense of calm, of security swept through her.

"Do you have siblings, Georgina?"

"Two older sisters," she replied.

"Do you have a good relationship with them?"

"I don't have any relationship with them."

"Why is that?"

Once again Georgina closed her eyes as ancient memories cascaded through her…bad memories…horrendous ones. "I don't have anything to do with any of my family because they were verbally, physically and emotionally abusive to me," she replied, despite the ever-stronger constriction in her chest.

"Why was that, Georgina?" Bob asked. "Were you a bad little girl?"

Alex's hand fell to her shoulder and even though she'd told him she wanted him to treat her only as a professional, she was grateful for the touch that kept her connected to the here and now as she darted down the rabbit hole where all her monsters lived.

"No, I wasn't a bad little girl. My problem was that I was born a girl. My sisters are four and five years older than me. When my mother got pregnant again my father was certain she was going to deliver him the son he desperately wanted. Instead he got me. He called me the abortion that should have happened."

She was vaguely aware of Alex's fingers tightening on her shoulder as she fought the demons of her past. The last thing she wanted to do was bare her skeletons in front of the team, in front of Alex, but she would do it if it helped further the investigation. She would give to Bob what she'd never been able to give to Alex or anyone else on the face of the earth.

She'd give him her nightmares.

It was as if Bob had poked a hole in a dam and now the flood of evil spilled from her in an emotional burst.

"Yeah, Bob, I had a crappy childhood. My father hated me and insisted that my mother and sisters have nothing to do with me. I was kicked and beaten by all of them when I wasn't locked in a closet for days at a time."

"I hear your pain, Georgina. I feel your pain," Bob said. "My old man was a mean drunk and he was drunk most of the time. I was beaten nearly every day of my life and my dear mother did nothing to stop it."

"Tell me, Bob, how did you manage to get the people you kidnapped?" Georgina asked. Despite the turmoil and chaos the discussion about her past had stirred up in her head, she hadn't lost track of her main goal—to get any information she could from him. "Did you take them alone or do you have a partner?"

Bob snorted. "I work alone. Partners only screw things up."

"So did you just surprise them and force them at gunpoint to go with you?" she asked.

"How pedestrian," he replied dryly. "Actually, the one thing my daddy taught me was how to blow poison darts. From our saggy little porch I could shoot a gator in the eye from ten feet out. Of course I didn't use poison for my victims. I used just enough tranquilizer to knock them out long enough for me to move them into their new homes. The drug has the aftereffect of loss of memory for several days, but that worked in my favor. Amberly and Cole were the most difficult because I had to keep them continuously drugged throughout the long road trip home."

Tim gave a thumbs-up, indicating that he'd managed to get the phone number and triangulate the call and had a location where it was coming from. Alex raced over to his computer, took a look and then headed for the door with a nod to Frank and Matt to go with him.

Georgina picked her phone up from the table and hurried after them. "How are you keeping all those people?" she asked, still connected to the call and knowing she needed to keep him talking for as long as possible.

"Very carefully," he said and then laughed, the sound shivering through her already fragile state.

"Let Macy go," she said, aware of the emotion that filled her throat, nearly stifled her voice. "I told you about my childhood. I did what you asked. Now you do something for me. Let her go."

"I've thought about it and I'm pleased that you shared so much with me, but I'm not ready to give up little Macy yet," he replied.

"Please let her go." She drew a deep breath in an effort to keep her emotions in check. "Let them all go."

"I think we've talked long enough for one day," Bob replied. "We'll talk again, sweet Georgina." He clicked off just as the four of them burst out of the building's back door.

As Frank and Matt raced toward Matt's car, Georgina hurried after Alexander toward his. "He hung up," she said unnecessarily as she slid into the passenger seat.

"The call came from the college campus. Let's hope he decides to linger for a while." Alex started the engine and squealed out of the parking lot and onto the street. He hit the button to start his flashing lights, zooming through the light traffic with Matt and Frank close behind.

She was grateful that Alexander didn't talk. She was

in a dark place that she hadn't visited for a very long time. Bob had managed to wrench memories from her she'd thought were long forgotten. He'd reminded her of what it had been like to be unwanted, unloved and unworthy.

It had only been when she'd joined the police force and then later the FBI that she'd found her worth, some form of self-respect and dignity, and the desire to be the very best that she could be at her job.

"The signal appeared to be coming from the bench area in front of the gym," Alex said as he braked to a halt at the curb by the college. Almost before the engine was completely off, he was out of the door and running.

Matt and Frank parked and ran after him while Georgina hurried out of the car and headed in the same direction. She hoped he was still there. She hoped and prayed that this was it, that they'd get him in custody and he'd tell them where he had his captives.

She picked up her pace, running after the men as her stomach rolled with the need to throw up and her brain continued to fire memories of her childhood through her head.

The men reached the area first, where four students were hanging out, two seated on the concrete bench and two standing.

"FBI. All of you put your hands up where we can see them," Alex said as he approached the group with his gun drawn.

The two young men who had been seated jumped to their feet and all of them raised their hands over their heads. "Wha...what's going on?" one of them asked.

Frank and Matt also had their guns drawn and the four were now circled by the agents.

"Very carefully, very easy, all of you get your cell phones out and set them on the bench," Alex instructed.

"This is about a cell phone?" A tall, dark-haired young man asked. "I've got it. It was sitting on the bench when we came out of the gym. I was going to turn it in to lost and found."

He reached into his shirt pocket and plucked out a cell phone and set it on the bench, then quickly raised his hand once again.

"How do we know that isn't your cell phone?" Georgina asked.

The young man gazed at the phone with scorn. "Look at it. It's a cheap piece of crap. It doesn't even have internet capabilities. I've got my own phone right here." He reached into the pocket of a duffel bag next to him and pulled out an expensive phone with all the bells and whistles.

He was here and now he was gone. The sick roll of Georgina's stomach intensified. As Alex questioned the young men, Matt pulled on latex gloves and put the phone in a plastic evidence bag he pulled from his pocket.

They would find nothing on the phone, she thought. Bob was far too smart to leave a phone for them to find unless he knew they'd glean nothing from it. It was a cheap throwaway and she knew he'd left it behind just to taunt them.

Before the men even finished speaking to the students, she turned and headed back to the car, her legs unsteady and a bitter taste in the back of her throat.

She got into the car, and a few minutes later Alex joined her. "Are you okay?" he asked.

"No. I think I need you to take me home. I'm requesting the rest of the day off." Her voice sounded tinny and as if it came from someplace far away.

Alex asked no questions. He started the car and headed in the direction of her house. He apparently sensed that she was in a place where she didn't want to talk, didn't want to listen, for he didn't speak until he pulled up into her driveway. He obviously knew that she'd be no good to anyone for the rest of the day.

"Are you sure you're going to be all right?"

She unbuckled her seat belt and opened the door. "I'll be fine by tomorrow morning. I just need some time alone right now." She got out of the car and shut the door, grateful that she could enter a code that would open the garage door and grant her entry into the house since she'd left her purse in the war room.

She didn't look back. As the garage door rose, she ducked under it and hurried to the door that would take her into her kitchen. She punched the button to close the garage door and then headed for the bathroom where she fell to the floor in front of the toilet and threw up.

She felt as if she was purging all the rage and grief that had been buried inside her for so long. Tears blurred her vision as she continued to be sick.

She hated Bob, not just for the crimes he'd committed but for what he'd done to her. He'd forced her back into a darkness she'd thought she'd escaped long ago. More than anything, she hated him for making her appear weak in front of her team.

When she was finally finished being sick, she pulled

herself to her feet, brushed her teeth and then went back into the living room and curled up on the sofa with the television on.

Tomorrow she'd be strong. Tomorrow she would be the kind of agent she needed to be, but right now she needed to deal with the fact that despite Alex's warnings to her, Bob had gotten into her head and brought up memories she needed to banish from her mind forever.

THE AFTERNOON CREPT BY slowly with Alexander's thoughts split between the case and the broken woman he'd dropped off earlier. He'd never seen Georgina so shattered and he worried that the conversation with their perp had pushed her over an edge he hadn't realized existed inside her.

He now knew why Georgina had never wanted to share anything of her past with him. He now recognized that she had demons inside her he couldn't begin to understand.

"Kind of a coincidence that the phone was found not far from where our kooky reporter lives," Matt said, pulling Alex back to the work at hand.

"He admitted freely that he'd been to all the crime scenes," Frank added. "Maybe he's our perp hiding in plain sight."

"Maybe," Alex replied absently. "Two things I think we can agree that we learned from the conversation Georgina had with Bob. The first is that he probably grew up in the swamps. He talked about blowing darts at gators when he was young. The second thing is that I think he's probably well educated."

"*Pedestrian* isn't a word that normally flows from

a thug's mouth," Terry replied. "Hell, I went to college and I've never used that word in a conversation in my life."

Nicholas walked through the door and Alexander suddenly realized the man had been missing for several hours. "Where in the hell have you been?" he demanded.

"I told everyone I was going to lunch," Nicholas replied defensively.

Alexander looked at his watch and then back at the dark-haired agent. "Since when do we get four-hour lunches around here?"

Nicholas's complexion took on a red cast. "I was only at lunch for half an hour. Then I got a call from a snitch who thought he had some information for us about this case, so I agreed to meet with him."

"And?"

"And the little jerk didn't have anything for me, he just wanted to see if I'd flip him a twenty. It was a waste of my time. What did I miss here?"

"Frank, fill him in," Alexander said and headed for the door. He walked down the hallway to the bathroom and once inside he sluiced cold water on his face and then dried off with a paper towel.

For just a moment as he'd faced Nicholas, he was too angry for words. He knew the younger agent had a reputation as being a lone wolf and had a desire to make a name for himself amid the ranks.

But Alexander had little use for somebody like that on this case. The task force was a unit that would function best as a single entity, with everyone knowing what everyone else was doing and learning.

He frowned at his reflection in the mirror. Had Nicholas ever been present when Georgina had received a call from Bob? No, Nicholas had always been absent when the calls came in.

Crazy. The thoughts that whirled through his mind were crazy. There was no way Nicholas could be responsible for the phone calls to Georgina. Alexander was definitely entertaining crazy thoughts.

He tossed the towel into the trash and then left the bathroom and returned to the war room, his anger back under control.

"Just a word to all of you," he said, although his focus was on Nicholas. "We are a team here and we work together as a team. I've assigned you all a partner and anything you're doing your partner should know about. No exceptions, got it?"

The men all murmured their assent and everyone got back to their assigned jobs. Alexander sat down and opened the folder he carried everywhere with him. It contained all the reports and photos from the previous disappearances and everything that the task force had done in this investigation.

He'd gotten word from the lab that none of the food that had been in Jackson's refrigerator had been tainted by anything, a point that didn't matter now that Bob had confessed how he'd taken his victims. Tranquilizer darts—it made sense given the fact that none of the victims had appeared to have had an opportunity to fight back.

"Tim and Jeff, focus in on all buildings that are near the swamps in the area. My gut says this guy will stay where things are familiar to him. Nicholas and Frank, focus in on any murders that occurred within the last ten years or so around the swamp areas. If he killed his parents at the old homestead, then I have a feeling that homestead is swampland."

"You know it's possible their murder was never reported," Jeff said. "Those swamp people are a tight-knit group that have little to do with law enforcement. Our perp might have killed his parents and fed their bodies to the gators."

"At this point anything is possible. Check missing persons reports during that time period. Surely somebody would notice if two people just went missing," Alex said.

Once again the room grew silent except for the clicking of computer keys. Alex stared down at the folder open in front of him. The photo that stared back at him was Macy's.

There was no question in his mind that Georgina had put herself through a terrible hell in an effort to please Bob enough that he would agree to release the little girl.

The bastard. His chest filled with pain as he thought of what Georgina had shared, as he realized how difficult it must have been for her to go back to such a horrendous time in her life, to dredge up memories that should have stayed buried deep in her mind.

Secrets. He'd always known she had secrets. He just hadn't realized they involved childhood abuse and neglect. There was no question that it bothered him more than a little bit that she would give that piece of herself to a killer, but had never shared any of it with him throughout their marriage.

He wondered how she was doing. He'd never seen

her so pale, so sickly looking in all the time he'd known her. He reached a hand to his pocket for his phone and then dismissed the idea of calling her.

She'd made it clear what she needed from him, and a check-in call wouldn't be considered appropriate under her conditions. Still, he couldn't help the worry that weighed on him as he thought of her at home all alone with only her demons as company.

"I've been checking Roger Cambridge and Michelle Davison since they've both been around the college in the last week," Frank said. "And I found a connection between the two of them that probably means nothing."

"What kind of connection?" Alexander asked, grateful for anything that would keep his mind focused on work and not on Georgina.

"It's weak, but they both took the same class in college, a class called Inside the Killer's Mind: Aberrant Behavior through Case Studies. It's taught by Professor Jacob Tanner."

"He was in front of Georgina and me in line at the book signing for Michelle," Alexander said and then frowned. "But I didn't pay much attention to him." Unfortunately he'd been far more focused on the author and her boyfriend than the man in line in front of him.

"I'll check in with Professor Tanner tomorrow. Maybe he can give me some insight into his former students," Alexander said.

"If Georgina isn't available to tag along with you tomorrow, I'd be happy to," Nicholas said.

"I'll decide who is going where in the morning," Alexander replied. He hoped that Georgina would be back, that today hadn't completely shattered her not only personally but professionally as well.

It was just after eight when he finally dismissed the team. After the room had emptied, Alexander remained, his mind trying to process everything that had occurred in the past eight hours.

Maybe Professor Tanner would be able to give them some insight into Michelle and Roger Dodger, the wonder reporter, some insight that might indicate whether either of them had the potential to be a killer.

It would be nice if Professor Tanner could provide an easy solve to this complicated case, but Alexander didn't hold out much hope for that.

The swamp reference had definitely been a lead to follow, but there were plenty of swamps in and around Baton Rouge. It could take weeks…months to check every building for the missing people.

And he wasn't sure he wanted Georgina taking any more of the creep's phone calls. It had gotten to her today. She'd given up too much of herself, sacrificed a piece of her soul in an effort to negotiate with Bob.

He had no idea if she'd be any use to the team now or not, but what concerned him more was her emotional well-being. He had a feeling she'd only shared a taste from the plate of horror that had been her childhood. How much more she must have gnawing holes deep inside her soul.

It was after nine when he finally left the FBI building with the need to drive around for a while and process everything the day had brought.

At least Georgina hadn't sacrificed herself for nothing. They now believed the man had been born and raised around the swamps and that somehow, some way, he'd become educated beyond what would be expected from a spawn of the swamp.

Either he was a self-educated person or he'd had some schooling additional to high school. Words were Michelle Davison's business. Roger appeared to be a fairly well-educated man. So neither of them could be taken off their list of suspects. He just had a feeling that neither of them were guilty of these crimes.

Of course, he knew Michelle hadn't physically carried out the kidnappings, but her boyfriend, Jax, would have been able to commit the crimes at her bidding or even unbeknownst to her.

He drove for about half an hour and was somehow unsurprised when he found himself pulling into Georgina's street. Darkness had fallen and he told himself he had no intention of stopping in to see her. He just needed to drive by her house and make himself feel better.

As he approached her house, his headlights fell on her front lawn where two people appeared to be fighting. He stopped his car, pulled his gun and got out. "Halt!" he yelled.

One of the figures froze, while the other fell to the ground. The one standing turned and ran and Alexander raced forward. From a nearby streetlight, he saw that it was Georgina on the ground.

"Go," she gasped. "I'm fine, just go catch him."

Alexander hesitated only a moment and then ran in the direction her attacker had gone. His heart beat frantically as a dog barked in the distance. He couldn't think about what might have happened had he not arrived at the scene when he did. He couldn't think about anything but catching whoever had attacked Georgina.

Still, what he wanted and reality were two different things. The darkness of the night played in the attacker's favor and the attacker had enough of a head start on Alexander that by the time he reached the next corner, he didn't know which way to go.

He stopped and listened. The only sound he heard was the frantic beat of his own heart. No footfalls, no crackling of brush or any new barks to indicate which direction the man had run.

He was gone, swallowed up by the night. With both frustration and worry boiling inside him, Alexander turned and hurried back down the sidewalk toward Georgina's house.

When he got there, she was no place to be seen and he breathed a sigh of relief as he realized she'd probably gone inside and locked the doors behind her.

He went up to the door and softly knocked. "Georgina, it's me."

She opened the door and before he could take a step inside she fell into his arms, sobbing and shaking. "It was him," she finally managed to gasp into the front of Alexander's shirt. "It was Bob. He wanted to add me to his collection."

Alexander tightened his arms around her and moved them both deeper into the living room, stunned by two things. He was surprised that Bob had confronted Georgina in a way that was not his normal mode of attack.

But equally as surprising was the fact that in all the years he'd known her, he had never seen Georgina cry.

Bob had gotten pieces of her past and now he'd gotten her tears. For those facts alone, if Alexander ever got the chance, he'd kill the man.

Chapter Eight

Georgina finally moved out of Alex's arms, deep sobs slowing as she sank down on the sofa. She raised her hands to her face and angrily swiped away the tears. She'd not only been terrified, she'd been stupid and the result had nearly been devastating.

She was aware of Alex sinking down next to her, his body warmth radiating out as the scent of his familiar cologne began to slowly calm her.

Dropping her hands to her lap, she turned to face him. "I was so stupid," she said angrily. "I fell for a ruse and I should have known better."

"Tell me what happened." His voice was soft and when he reached for one of her hands, she allowed the contact, needing the warmth of his touch.

"I was asleep on the sofa and I woke up and heard a baby crying. It was such a plaintive wail and it sounded like it was coming from just outside my front door. I was still half asleep, but I decided I needed to check it out. I opened the door, stepped out on the porch and that's when he grabbed me." A new sob escaped her as she thought of that moment when strong arms had wrapped around her and a voice had whispered in her ear.

"The minute he grabbed me, he whispered that I would be the queen of his collection." She shuddered and Alexander squeezed her hand more tightly.

"Were you able to get any kind of description of him?"

She shook her head. "He had on a ski mask so I couldn't make out any facial features, but he was tall and very strong. If you hadn't come along when you did, he would have had me. I fought against him, but eventually he would have won the fight."

Alex frowned. "I wonder why he didn't take you like the others? With some sort of tranquilizer?"

"He said I was special, that I deserved special treatment because we'd shared so much." Once again a shiver rippled through her as she thought of how close she'd been to disappearing, of becoming the eighth person in his den.

"Dammit, we should have seen this coming," Alex said. "I should have known he'd come after you."

She disengaged her hand from his and gazed at him curiously. "Why are you here? Did you have any idea that I might be in trouble?"

"No, I was just driving around for a while before going home and you were on my mind so I decided to drive by your house."

"Your timing was impeccable," she replied and then released a tremulous sigh. "I've been through a lot of things in my life, but I don't think I've ever been as scared as when he grabbed me."

Alex stood and gazed down at her. "Pack your bags. You're coming home with me."

"Okay," she replied, obviously surprising him if the

look on his face was any indication. She stood. "I might be hardheaded, Alex, but I'm no fool. I feel the target on my head and I'm not about to make it easy for him by staying here all alone. I'll be right back with my bags."

She left the living room and went into her bedroom, where she pulled a suitcase from the closet and began to fill it with enough clothing to last a week or so. After that time they'd have to figure out what to do next where she was concerned.

She didn't particularly like the idea of spending time with Alex in the house they had once called home together, but she liked the alternative less.

She didn't have a security system here. She would be vulnerable to another attack if she stayed, and the next time she might not be so lucky.

As she left the bedroom and went into the bathroom to gather up toiletries, she told herself she would rather put up with the memories that being in that house with Alex would evoke than be Bob's next victim.

Within twenty minutes Alex was carrying the big suitcase out her front door and she followed behind with a smaller overnight bag.

She didn't feel completely safe until she was in his car and he was behind the wheel and pulling away from the curb. Over and over again, Bob's voice played in her head. "He spoke to me, but his voice was more a guttural growl than a real voice. I'm not sure I'd recognize it again if I heard him speaking normally."

"I hope you never get close enough to him to hear his voice again unless he's in handcuffs," Alex replied, his voice bearing the deep rumble of a papa bear protecting a cub. "I don't want you talking to him anymore."

She stared at him in surprise. His chiseled features were taut with tension in the glow from the dashboard. "Don't be silly. Of course I intend to talk to him again."

"Georgina, he got to you today. He got deep into your head." Alex didn't try to mask the deep worry in his voice.

"I know. You're right," she replied, knowing that to try to lie to him would be foolish, given what he'd heard on the phone conversation and her reaction afterward.

"I was afraid I'd lost you, that he'd pushed you too far over the edge."

She frowned and stared out the passenger window, remembering the traumatic conversation with Bob. "For a minute he did, he cast me back to a place I never wanted to revisit. But I just needed some time away from it all. I would have been fine by morning."

He didn't say anything and she had a feeling he didn't quite believe her. But she would have been fine. She would have been ready to face her job once again. After all, the job was the only thing she'd ever really trusted.

For the remainder of the drive, they were silent. She had no idea what was going on in Alex's head, but her head was filled with the feel of those strong arms around her, the low hiss of words meant to terrify and the scent of evil that had swelled in the air.

She'd fought him. She'd fought hard, but he'd been so much stronger, and if he'd had only another minute or two, he would have overwhelmed her and carried her away.

God, would she ever be warm again? The intimate contact with the killer and imagining what might have happened had Alex not come along had iced her insides to arctic levels.

A new tension, along with gratitude, filled her as they reached the house and Alex punched the button to raise the garage door.

She was walking back into her past by coming here. It was a past that had been filled with happiness, passion and ultimately the pain of self-realization. Still, she knew she'd be safe here. The house had a security system and an armed and dangerous Alex, who would never let danger come close to her again.

"I'll just put your bags in the guest room," he said as they walked out of the garage and into the kitchen. Georgina followed behind him, stunned to see that the kitchen looked exactly the same way it had on the day she'd walked away.

Nothing had changed and as she walked into the living room she realized nothing had changed there either. He hadn't redone the decor or bought new furniture. He hadn't even taken down their wedding picture that sat on the bookcase next to his criminal investigation books.

She followed him down the hallway to the second bedroom where he placed her suitcase and smaller bag on the floor. "You know where everything is and if you can't find something just let me know. How about I put on some coffee?"

"Actually, what I'd like most right now is a long hot bath and then sleep." She didn't want to sit at the table and rehash the night's events. She just wanted to get warm and feel safe.

She wanted to sleep without dreams, suffer no nightmares of Bob or her childhood and wake up ready to tackle the job once again. The job would keep her sane.

"Why don't we just say goodnight now," she continued. "It's already getting late and we can talk in the morning on the way to work."

He hesitated a moment and then nodded. "Okay, then I guess I'll just tell you good-night now and see you in the morning."

"Good night, Alex. And thanks for being at the right place at the right time."

"My pleasure," he replied with a smile.

She closed the bedroom door, as if to ward off the way his smile made her feel just a little shaky, just a little more vulnerable than she already felt.

She pulled her suitcase up on the bed and opened it, quickly hanging what needed to be hung and then throwing her underwear into one of the empty drawers in the dresser.

Don't think, she commanded herself. *Don't think about what might have happened if Alex hadn't appeared in the night. Don't think about the distant past and all the pain. Just breathe and keep your head empty of all thoughts.*

She grabbed her nightshirt, a pair of panties and her toiletry bag and went across the hall into the guest bathroom. There was another full bath in the master suite so she knew there was no reason for Alex to interrupt her.

She started the water in the tub and then began to undress, eager to get off the blouse and slacks that *he'd* touched. She wanted to scrub away any skin that had touched his. She felt him everywhere on her and she just wanted to scrub him off.

With the tub filled, she turned off the water and stepped into the heated depths. She sank down so that the hot water surrounded her to the shoulders, hoping to heat the inner core of ice that remained inside her.

Closing her eyes, she willed herself to relax, but her thoughts worked against her. How had he found out where she lived? Probably the same way he'd found out her cell phone number. There had to be a mole somewhere in the department. But it was difficult to believe that anyone in the agency would want to see the kidnapping or death of another agent.

As far as she knew she'd made no enemies in her five years as an FBI agent. Granted, she wasn't close to anyone, but she'd always gone out of her way to be pleasant to everyone she worked with.

Don't think, she told herself once again. She wouldn't be worth anything in the morning if she didn't relax and get a good night's sleep. And she wanted to be on her game the next day for she was certain that Bob would contact her again. He'd revel in the fact that he had gotten so close to her.

She shivered and realized the hot water wasn't working, that the core of ice inside her remained. It took only a few minutes for her to use the minty scented soap and scrub herself clean. She sank completely under and then rose up and stepped out of the tub and grabbed a fluffy towel from the cabinet.

When dried, she pulled on her nightgown and panties, finger-combed her damp hair and then left the bathroom and scurried back across the hall. The house was silent and dark, letting her know that Alex had already gone to bed.

It felt strange to be getting into the bed in the guest room. She'd never slept in here before. She'd decorated the room in deep rich browns and tans and had thought it looked quite inviting at the time. But at this moment she only felt cold, afraid and lonely.

"Don't even think about it," she muttered to herself as she punched her pillow. She shouldn't even think about the fact that Alex was just down the hall, that he'd been the one person who had always been able to warm her and make her feel safe and secure.

Going to him now would be one of the biggest mistakes she would ever make in her life. It would definitely give him the wrong impression.

Of course, she could make sure he didn't get the wrong impression. She could tell him that she just needed him for one night, wanted him to hold her and make love to her to banish everything else from her mind.

She would be using him for this night to drive from her mind everything that had happened in the last twelve hours, but as long as she was up front with him about it, then surely he couldn't hold it against her.

She knew she was making a mistake when she got out of the bed. She knew it was a mistake as she made her way down the darkened hallway.

She hesitated in front of his closed bedroom door, knowing that if she knocked there would be no going back. While she could justify this night in her mind, she would never be able to take it back.

Once she knocked on the door, she knew he'd invite her into his bed and she knew they would make love. But before that happened she had to let him know that it was just tonight, not a new beginning for them, not a second chance, just a single moment of need that would never again be repeated.

She raised her hand and, drawing a deep breath, she knocked on the door.

AT FIRST ALEXANDER THOUGHT he'd only imagined the faint knock on his door because he wanted her to come to him. It was only when he heard a second, louder knock that he responded. "Come in," he called, his heart pounding a little faster.

His door opened, and in the faint moonlight casting in through his windows he could see her silhouette in the doorway. "Did I wake you?" she asked.

"No, I'm not even close to being asleep," he replied. "Did you need something?" His voice sounded slightly hoarse to his own ears as his blood rushed through his body.

"I need you."

Her voice sounded stark and his heart pressed painfully tight against his chest. "You've got me, Georgina. Whenever you need me, you've always had me."

She remained standing, as if weighing her options. "It's just for tonight, Alex. I'm using you. I'm only inviting myself into your bed for tonight, not back into your life in any meaningful way."

Although it wasn't what he wanted to hear, he wanted her badly enough to agree to any terms she'd set into place. "So you just want to take advantage of me for a single night," he said with a forced lightness.

"That's about the size of it," she replied.

"Then what are you waiting for?"

She flew across the room and landed on top of him like a long-legged nymph seeking home. Despite everything that had happened through the long day, he laughed with the sheer joy of holding her in his arms once again.

As she crawled beneath the sheets to join him, it was as if the past two years without her had only been a bad dream and now she was back where she belonged.

They lay side by side, facing each other and in the moonlight her eyes glowed with the fire of want, of need.

He reached for her and she filled his arms as their lips met in a fiery kiss. Alexander had two years of desire built up inside him and he gave her that emotion by delving his tongue to dance with hers.

She wrapped her arms around his neck and pulled herself half on his chest as their mouths remained melded together. Someplace in the back of his mind he knew she was giving him no more than her body. She'd always been generous with that, but she'd never been able to achieve any real intimacy with him outside of the bedroom. He would never really have her heart. She kept that so closely guarded.

He shoved this thought away as he focused on the here and now. These moments of this night were all he had and he wanted to savor each and every one.

She slid her hands up and down his naked chest and pulled her mouth from his to nuzzle into the hollow of his throat. His hands glided down her back to the edge of her nightshirt. He was already fully erect, ready to tear her nightshirt over her head, pull her panties off and take her as he'd never taken her before.

But he didn't do any of those things. He knew it was important that he let her set the pace, nonverbally telling him what she needed and when. It was a lack of control that had driven her to his bed. He knew instinctively that he needed to allow her to be in total control now.

She sat up and pulled her nightshirt over her head and tossed it to the floor, then straddled him and leaned forward to kiss him again, her bare breasts against his bare chest.

The contact was immensely pleasurable as she plied his mouth with heat and hunger and her nipples pebbled hard against his skin.

The only thing keeping them from complete intimate contact was his boxers and her panties, but she seemed in no hurry to take them off as her lips once again trailed from his mouth, down his jawline and then over his chest.

He was in a dream that he hoped would never end, a dream he'd had a thousand times since the day she'd left him. She sat up and he reached to cup her breasts, paying special attention to her hard nipples, and was rewarded by a low, deep moan that escaped her lips.

He wanted her moaning. He wanted to make it impossible for her to ever want another man. She was all he'd ever wanted, all he'd ever needed and he loved her as he would never love another woman.

She rolled off him just long enough for her to remove her panties and at the same time he quickly shimmied down his boxers and kicked them off.

When she straddled him once again, all he could think about was burying himself in her, possessing her completely for the length of time he could control himself, for the length of time she'd allow him.

As if reading his thoughts, she grasped his hard length and then guided him into her. As she sank down, she once again moaned with pleasure.

He tensed, trying to maintain control as her tight moistness surrounded him. She looked beautiful in the moonlight and he had to close his eyes to focus on not letting go too soon.

"Now I feel warm and safe," she whispered.

Whatever words he might have said in response vanished as she began to rock her hips back and forth. The friction of her movements shot blood through his veins, stole every other thought from his mind.

She gasped and began to move faster and he knew she was on the verge of a climax. He thrust upward, wanting her there before he lost all semblance of control.

And then she was there, shuddering uncontrollably as she half laughed, half cried out his name. His own control snapped and wave after wave of pleasure jolted through him as he found his own release.

She collapsed on his chest, utterly boneless against him as their breathing found a more normal rhythm. She finally raised her head to look at him. "I'm not sure I have the energy to move."

"Then stay right where you are." He stroked his hands down her slender bare back and wished they never had to move again.

"Do you mind if I sleep in here with you?" she asked. "Just this one night," she added as if wanting to remind him that this was a one-shot deal.

"Do you really think I'm going to tell you no?" he replied wryly.

"I'll be right back." She slid off the bed and disappeared down the hallway to the bathroom. He got up and went into the master bath and then found his boxers on the floor and pulled them back on.

He was back in the bed when she returned to his room. She pulled her nightshirt over her head and then got beneath the sheets and snuggled against him.

He stroked her short, silky hair and closed his eyes, wishing the night would never end. Unfortunately, as far as he was concerned, the night was far too short. He awakened just before five to a dark room and the other side of the bed empty.

He pulled on a white robe that he'd gotten when he and Georgina had taken a cruise for their honeymoon and followed the scent of freshly brewed coffee down the hallway.

She sat in the chair at the table where she'd always sat in the mornings when she'd lived here. She was still clad in her nightshirt, her hair a spiky mess that only made her more beautiful to him.

She smiled at him. "You're up early."

"You're up earlier." He got a cup of coffee and joined her at the table. There was a sense of déjà vu about the scene. They had always begun their mornings with coffee at this table, with her in her nightshirt and him in his robe. "Bad dreams?"

She shook her head. "No, I just woke up and couldn't go back to sleep. Instead of fighting it, I decided to go ahead and get up." She frowned. "Did I wake you up?"

"No, I woke up on my own." He curled his fingers

around his coffee mug, unsure where to take the conversation next. He knew she certainly didn't want any morning-after chatter.

"We need to check everyone's alibi for last night," she said, letting him know she'd been thinking about the case. "I know the person who tried to grab me was a man, so Michelle doesn't need an alibi, but her boyfriend does."

"I'll get everyone on the alibi situation as soon as we get to work. In the meantime, yesterday evening we decided it might be a good idea to talk to Professor Jacob Tanner."

"Why does that name sound familiar?" she asked.

"He was in line in front of us at Michelle's book signing," Alexander replied.

"That's right. I remember Michelle greeting him." She paused and took a sip of her coffee. "So, why are we interested in talking to him?"

"We found out that he taught both Michelle and Roger in a class about killers and aberrant behavior. We thought maybe he might be able to give us some insight into the two."

"You mean you want to ask him if either one of them were bed-wetters, fire-starters or into torturing small animals?" she asked teasingly.

He grinned, knowing she'd just named what were supposed to be three precursors to becoming a serial killer. In his years of chasing killers, he had yet to find a bed-wetter among the group. "You never know what he might remember about those two, and right now he's just a straw for us to grasp in hopes that something fresh will come out of it."

For the next thirty minutes he caught her up on everything that had occurred the day before after she'd left. The fact that there was so little to tell her cast a pall of frustration through him.

Even more frustrating was the fact that the perp had come so close to grabbing Georgina last night. Thank God he hadn't succeeded, but Alexander should have managed to catch him. He could have ended it all last night if he'd just run a little faster, if he'd just tried a little harder.

He stared at Georgina, now cast in the glow of the morning sunrise. A fist of tension balled up in his chest. "After what nearly happened last night, we're going to be stuck together like glue."

"I know I'm a target now," she said. "But, what happened after what nearly happened last night isn't going to happen again."

Her sentence would have been quite confusing to anyone else, but he knew she was telling him that she wouldn't be sharing his bed again. When she'd said one night only, she'd meant it.

He would have to live with that. What he couldn't live with was somehow screwing up and causing danger to grab Georgina. He couldn't go through another Kelly Gilmer failure, especially with the woman he loved as yet another victim.

Chapter Nine

"Last night our perp tried to grab Georgina," Alexander said.

It was seven o'clock in the morning and everyone was in the war room. When Alexander made his first announcement to the group, everyone turned to look at Georgina.

"I just happened to be driving by her place and saw her grappling with Bob in her front yard. He ran when I pulled up and I tried to follow, but lost him in the darkness. What I want everyone focused on today is getting alibis as to where Jax, Michelle and Roger were last night between the hours of nine and ten. I want the alibis checked and rechecked."

"Aren't Michelle and Jax on some book tour?" Nicholas asked.

"Yes, and according to the itinerary I got from Michelle's agent, they were supposed to be in New Orleans all day yesterday and until tomorrow. She has a signing there tonight."

"It's only about an hour and a half drive from New Orleans to here. They could have driven back here, attacked Georgina and been back at their hotel by midnight."

"And Roger doesn't do his news show on Wednesday nights so he could have been anywhere last night," Terry said.

"I want to know where *anywhere* was," Alexander replied. "Right now Roger and Jax are the only halfway viable suspects we have. I particularly want to know Jax's whereabouts last night since we now know his parents died in a house fire about ten years ago. Do we have any more information about that fire?"

"I checked all the records from the investigation and it was definitely arson. Jax was at the top of the suspect list but was a hundred miles away when the fire occurred and the authorities could never make anything stick. The case remains open, but hasn't been worked in years," Matt said.

"It still just could be a coincidence that Bob told Georgina he killed his parents and Jax's parents died in an arson fire," Nicholas said. "Or Bob could have been lying about everything he told Georgina."

"He wasn't lying," she replied. Despite everything she had endured the day before, this morning she looked cool and confident.

"How can you be so sure?" Nicholas asked.

"Trust me, I know he was telling the truth. We're looking for somebody who grew up with abuse and trauma in his childhood. He's filled with rage and, according to his own words, has visions of becoming the greatest serial killer of all time. But he's also tightly controlled, a planner and a very organized kidnapper/killer and that will make him even more difficult to find."

She drew a deep breath and glanced around with a

faint blush. "Sorry, I didn't mean to go into a long, boring monologue."

Alexander smiled at her. "Not boring, definitely things we all need to keep in mind." His smile fell as he glanced around at the members of the team. "We also think he's well educated, probably has a good job and may even be married and have a family."

"This isn't your ordinary thug," Frank added. "He's managed to remain elusive in two different cities, at two different crime scenes."

"Right now my money is on Roger Cambridge," Nicholas replied. "He has photos and reports about each crime that he shouldn't have. He's admitted to being in both Mystic Lake and Bachelor Moon."

"I just want to know where he was last night when Georgina was attacked, and I don't want you all making phone calls to the persons of interest," Alexander said. "Frank, Matt and Nicholas, I want the three of you to take off for New Orleans. Check and double-check on Michelle and Jax. If they said they ate at a particular restaurant, then you go to the restaurant and confirm it."

He turned his gaze toward Terry. "I want you to rattle Roger's cage, and Jeff and Tim, you continue to work on potential locations in and around swamp areas." He paused and then sat down. "What are you all waiting for?"

It took only minutes for the room to clear out, leaving behind only Alexander, Georgina, Tim and Jeff. "Grab some coffee and relax, it's too early for us to head over to the college campus," he said to Georgina.

"I'm coffeed out," she replied. "Tim, how is the search going of the buildings you've located?"

He frowned. "The locals have checked out about thirty locations and found nothing. They're being very cooperative, but there are also a lot of empty warehouses and buildings in and around the swamplands."

"Eventually you'll stumble on the needle in the haystack," Georgina said with a warm smile to the younger agent.

The tip of Tim's ears turned pink. "Thanks. Let's just hope I find the place before the student decides he's learned all he can from his teacher captives."

Georgina's eyes held the same kind of horror that rippled through Alexander at Tim's words. It struck home again that if the seven kidnapped people were still alive, it was only because Bob allowed them to live.

He had the power to keep them as captives or kill them, and there was no way any of the team could guess when Bob would decide that his captives were more hindrance than help.

Alexander knew he was working against a ticking clock and he had no idea when the clock would strike the time that people would die. And the team had so little to go on in finding those people and the man who would end their lives when he decided.

It was just before nine when Alexander and Georgina parked in one of the college lots behind the Division of Humanities building. In this building, students learned philosophy, psychology and criminal justice. It was also in this building that Dr. Jacob Tanner taught his classes and had his office.

"West wing, second floor," Alexander said as they entered the front door along with several students. While they had waited for it to be late enough to come to the college, he had done some background digging into Jacob Tanner.

The professor was highly esteemed and his classes were the most popular among the students. He was only thirty-two years old but had zoomed through his education and had gotten his job teaching here four years ago. He lived alone in an upscale townhouse near the college and liked to play chess and bridge with fellow teachers.

"I don't know if he'll remember Roger, but we know he definitely has maintained some sort of contact with Michelle," Georgina said as they took the stairs to the second floor. "I wonder if he had any contact at all with Michelle's boyfriend."

"We should have checked records to see if Jax attended college here. To be honest, it didn't occur to me. He doesn't exactly read as a college-educated man."

"Maybe he's fooling us with his brawn act. Maybe Michelle likes a smart man when it comes to mental stimulation, but likes a thug as a bodyguard and in the bedroom," Georgina replied.

"Would you like a thug in the bedroom?" Alexander asked.

She shot him a dirty look. "You know exactly what I like in the bedroom, Alex, and we're not taking this particular conversation any further."

He liked the way her cheeks flamed with color. She might have told him that last night was an anomaly that wouldn't happen again, but she wasn't as immune to him as she wanted him to believe.

They easily found Professor Tanner's office, and Alexander knocked on the door. "Just a minute," a woman's voice drifted through the door. He exchanged a glance with Georgina who shrugged. Maybe the professor was important enough to warrant a secretary.

The door opened to reveal a young woman with wheat-colored hair that was pulled back into a severe bun, and she was clad in tailored slacks and blouse. She looked as if she were desperate to appear older than she was.

"May I help you?" she asked.

"We're looking for Professor Tanner," Alexander said.

"He's not in yet. I'm Megan James, his student assistant. Is there something I can help you with?" Her smile was cool and professional.

"When do you expect Dr. Tanner to be in?" Alexander asked.

"In about fifteen minutes or so. He has a nine-thirty class."

Georgina displayed her badge. "Then we'll just come in and wait for him." She didn't give the young assistant any opportunity to protest, but instead pushed past her and into the room.

Alexander followed as Megan stepped back. Jacob Tanner had a cushy office, with a bank of windows that looked out on trees and green space. There was a small desk, neat and tidy, and a love seat in hunter green.

The walls held wildlife photos, but it was the bookcase behind the desk that drew his attention. Abnormal psychology books lined one shelf, the collection impressive. The other shelves held books on Ted Bundy, John Wayne Gacy, Jeffrey Dahmer and all the notorious serial killers through time. There were even several books about Jack the Ripper.

"Is Professor Tanner in some kind of trouble?" Megan asked worriedly as she gestured for them to sit on the love seat.

"No, nothing like that. We just have a few questions to ask him."

Megan sank down in the chair at the desk. "That's good, because he's the best. All the students love him, and his classes are always the first ones to fill up." It was obvious Megan had a bad case of hero worship going on.

"How is he to work for?" Alexander asked, just passing time.

"Wonderful. He's so patient and kind, and it's been an honor for me to learn from and work for him." She smiled beatifically.

The door opened and the man of the hour walked in. Megan jumped out of his chair behind the desk while Georgina and Alexander rose simultaneously from the love seat.

"What's this? Some kind of a welcoming committee?" Jacob Tanner cast the two agents a pleasant smile. He was tall, medium weight, with dusty-blond hair and blue eyes. He was handsome in a boyish way, which was probably what made him a favorite among the female students on campus.

"They're FBI agents," Megan said. "They want to talk to you."

"Oh, okay." Tanner didn't appear concerned. "Megan, why don't you go on downstairs to the theater and make sure the podium and video equipment is ready to go for today's classes."

Once the young woman had left the room, Tanner

closed the door behind her and walked over to his desk chair. "Please," he said, gesturing them back down on the love seat as he sat. Official introductions were made. "What is it that you think I can help you with?"

"We saw you at Michelle Davison's book signing last week and from what we understand she was a student of yours," Alexander said.

Tanner nodded. "One of the brightest I think I've ever taught. Is she in some kind of trouble?"

"She's a person of interest in a case we're working on. What do you know about her boyfriend, Jax White?" Georgina asked.

Seated so close to her on the love seat, Alexander was surrounded by Georgina's scent and he tried hard to ignore it and focus on Tanner, who had a look on his face as if he'd tasted something unpleasant.

"Jax was also a student of mine. He barely passed my class and I don't think he actually graduated. He was bright enough but unmotivated. Michelle could do much better when it comes to boyfriends."

"What about Roger Cambridge? We understand he also took several of your classes," Alexander stated.

Tanner leaned back in his chair and smiled in open amusement. "Roger Cambridge. He was a good student, he never missed a class, but he also loved to draw attention to himself. He wanted to make sure everyone knew Roger Cambridge. I'm not surprised that he's doing his cheesy internet show. He desperately wants his fifteen minutes of fame."

"Enough to kidnap FBI agents and make the news so that he can report the news?" Georgina asked.

Tanner's brow creased. "Roger was intense. He really

got into the classes, sought extra time with me to discuss various elements of the serial killers we studied in class. Do I think he's capable of committing a crime?" He leaned forward and shrugged. "To be honest, I don't know."

"We understand that your classes are some of the most popular that are offered," Georgina said.

He leaned back again and smiled. "You have to admit there is something fascinating about the criminal mind and what men and women are capable of doing to each other. In the classes, we explore the nature versus nurture theory and we go into details of some of the most infamous serial killers."

"Do you have any students now that ring bells of having the potential to commit crimes?" Georgina asked.

Tanner laughed. "I have to admit that I'm sure there are some maladjusted, troubled young people who are drawn to the class because of their own issues. Can I forecast who of those students will go on to become killers? Absolutely not. It would be nice for everyone if I could easily identify any students who would go on to commit violent crimes."

He looked at his watch and stood. "I'm afraid I need to leave. I've got a class to teach. Is there anything else I can help you with?"

"No, but if we think of something we'll get back in touch with you." Alexander and Georgina stood and together the three of them left the office.

"Good luck to both of you, and I'm sorry I couldn't be more help," Tanner said as they walked down the hallway toward the stairs. "I once considered becoming a police officer, but then I thought of the danger involved and changed my mind. Those who can, do, but those who can't, teach, right?" He gave them another pleasant smile and then hurried ahead of them and disappeared through a doorway.

"Well, that was a big waste of time," Alexander said in frustration as he and Georgina left the building and headed for his car. "He wasn't able to help us at all."

"Maybe not, but I found it interesting that he remembered Roger and Jax. It's obviously been several years since they were in his classes and Tanner has had hundreds of students since then." Georgina stopped talking long enough to get into the passenger seat and then resumed when he was behind the wheel.

"Maybe it's time we dug a little deeper into Roger, maybe put a tail on him. If he's looking for his fifteen minutes of fame, maybe he is our man," she said.

"Maybe," he agreed. "We'll see what the others have as far as alibis for last night on everyone. Roger better hope he has a damn airtight one."

He tightened his hands on the steering wheel. "What really worries me is that we don't even have Bob on our radar, that he's not Roger or Jax, but rather somebody we haven't even come into contact with other than the phone calls to you."

"Those phone calls will be his downfall," she said. "Somehow, someway, I'll get him to give up some useful information that will lead to his arrest."

Alexander frowned. "Not at the price you paid yesterday."

"Whatever it takes for success," she replied. "He won't get into my head again, but I need to keep the conversation with him going. It might be our only chance."

He glanced at her long enough to see the tension that tightened her features and then looked back at the road. "Why didn't you tell me about your childhood?" It had been a question that had plagued him since he'd listened to her talking about it to Bob.

"It was ugliness I hoped I had left in my past. I certainly didn't want to bring it into our marriage," she replied. She looked out the passenger window as if in an attempt to disengage from the conversation.

However, it was a conversation Alexander intended to have. "It was important for me to know about, Georgina. Your childhood is so much a part of what you become as an adult."

"I didn't want you to know that part of me. I just wanted to forget the way I was treated as a child. I left it behind when Child Protective Services took me away from my parents when I was sixteen."

Alexander shot her a look of surprise. "You went into foster care?"

She sighed and turned to look at him. "For two years I lived with a family who taught me what normal life was supposed to be like. They explained to me that what I'd suffered was called scapegoat child abuse. It's over and done with, and I survived and I don't want to talk about it anymore."

I survived. Alexander played her words over and over again in his mind. She said that it was fine, that she'd survived, but had she really?

He thought of all the times in their marriage when she'd been emotionally distant, as if she was afraid to trust him, afraid to love him with all her heart and soul.

If he'd known this information, maybe he would have

been able to figure out exactly what she needed from him. Maybe he would have been able to find the core of pain that must still reside inside her and soothe it, override it with all his love. Maybe if he'd known what she'd been through in her early life, he would have been able to stop her from leaving him.

Too late now, a little voice whispered in the back of his head. He'd obviously let her down, not been enough, and she'd made it clear to him that there were no do-overs where the two of them were concerned.

He'd always believed her to be one of the strongest women he'd ever known. Learning about what she'd endured had only solidified that belief. Still, he knew that everybody had a breaking point. He'd seen Georgina momentarily break yesterday, letting him know that she was vulnerable.

Now not only did he have to worry about catching Bob and finding the missing, he also had to be concerned about Georgina's physical safety and her mental state.

He didn't want the price of cracking this case to be damage to Georgina's fragile state of mind while playing a game with the killer.

Chapter Ten

The afternoon crawled by. Georgina once again found herself going through the files pertaining to the disappearance of Sam, Daniella and little Macy in Bachelor Moon, of Amberly and her husband Cole from Mystic Lake and everything they had about the disappearance of Jackson and Marjorie from Jackson's home.

She flipped the pages, looking for something, anything they might have missed, all the while acutely aware of her cell phone on the table before her.

As the afternoon progressed, the members of the team that Alexander had tasked with checking alibis began to return to report back what they'd found.

Although Michelle lived on the outskirts of New Orleans, she and Jax had spent the night in a hotel not far from the bookstore where she would be signing books tonight. They both had been seen in the New Orleans hotel dining room around seven the night before, but then hadn't been seen by anyone again until this morning. According to them, they had retired to their room and hadn't left, which meant neither of them had been cleared concerning the attack on Georgina.

The report on Roger's whereabouts at the time of

the attempted kidnapping of Georgina was also not a solid alibi. According to Roger, he'd had dinner with a couple of friends at the Pig Roast, a barbecue place near the campus, but they'd parted ways around seven and Roger had gone home, where he said he worked on notes for his next newscast and then went to bed.

The agents had confirmed that Roger did, indeed, meet friends for dinner at the Pig Roast, but couldn't confirm that he was at his apartment for the rest of the night.

So nobody had been cleared and the frustration of the team was evident in the silence that prevailed in the war room. The silence was broken only by the occasional cracking of Matt's knuckles.

"For crying out loud, stop that," Frank finally said when Matt popped his knuckles for the fifth time. "Don't you know that's not healthy."

"It's not hurting me," Matt protested.

"It's hurting me," Frank exclaimed. "It's making me freaking crazy."

"Okay, why don't we call it a day," Alex said. "It's after five, and I'm sure some of you would like to actually eat dinner with your families. We'll meet again at seven in the morning."

There was a stampede to the door as the men took off. It had been a long stretch for all of them without much time off.

"It's a good thing I wasn't standing near the door when I told them to take off for the night," Alex said dryly. "I would have been nothing but roadkill."

Georgina laughed, despite her general feeling of disappointment. She picked up her phone from the table and dropped it into her purse. "I'd hoped to hear from him today."

"You still might," Alex replied.

"I don't know. All the calls have come in during the afternoons." She started for the door, but paused as Alex didn't move.

She looked at him and he raked a hand through his hair and stared at her for a long moment. "Have you noticed that whenever you get a call from Bob, Nicholas is never around?"

She looked at him in stunned surprise. "As much as I dislike Nicholas, surely you aren't suggesting that he has anything to do with all of this."

"Crazy, right? I'm having crazy thoughts." He ushered her out of the room and into the hallway. "Just forget I said anything about it. You want to grab something to eat out or fix something at home?"

"Let's just cobble something together at home," she replied. "I don't really feel like going out. I'm ready for comfy clothes and an early night."

"Sounds good to me."

As they rode the elevator down to the first floor and then left the building and headed for his car, Georgina couldn't forget what Alex had said about Nicholas.

She brewed his words around in her head while they drove home and once there while she changed into a pair of sweatpants and a T-shirt.

She was in the kitchen with the refrigerator door open, trying to decide what to fix to eat when Alex joined her. He'd also pulled on a pair of black sweatpants and a matching T-shirt. He looked more relaxed than he had all day.

"Finding anything worthwhile in there?" he asked.

"We're looking at a soup and sandwich night or omelets with bacon and toast," she replied. She grabbed the bacon package. "And I know your love affair with bacon."

He laughed and grabbed a frying pan from the cabinet and set it on the stovetop. "Remember how we used to wrap bacon around hot dogs, or water chestnuts for a little cocktail snack in the evenings?"

She handed him the package of bacon. "I remember a lot of things we used to do." She consciously willed away the memory of those impromptu cocktail hours that almost always ended with the two of them making love. She didn't want to remember the good times. It hurt. The memories of being with Alex were almost as painful as her childhood memories, although for much different reasons.

She turned back to the refrigerator and pulled out the eggs, milk, cheese, a green pepper and an onion. For the next few minutes the only sound was the sizzling of bacon cooking and her cutting up the vegetables.

She couldn't let Alex get into her head, with memories of happiness and passion, with memories of laughter and love. There was no way she would return to his bed again tonight no matter how hard he subtly worked to turn her resolve into capitulation.

They worked in an easy companionship. Once the bacon was crisply fried, Alex made coffee and then moved to the toaster while she poured the omelet mixture into the waiting skillet.

It wasn't until they were seated across from each other at the kitchen table that she brought up what he'd said to her earlier. "What do we really know about Nicholas's background?"

"Not much," he admitted. "He doesn't talk about his past."

She crunched into a piece of bacon and then followed it with a drink of coffee. "He's very ambitious," she said as she set her cup back down.

Alex raised a dark eyebrow. "Ambitious enough to commit these crimes, then get himself on a task force and then what?"

"I don't know, set somebody else up to take the fall. Be the hero. You're the one who put the idea into my head in the first place."

He grinned. "I know, but I really expected you to tell me I was crazy. I didn't expect you to actually entertain the idea."

She cut into her omelet and then met his gaze once again. "Unfortunately, I don't much like Nicholas and maybe it's my negative feelings toward him coming into play. But, truthfully, I'm not sure I trust him. I'm not sure what he might be capable of in an effort to make a name for himself in the department."

Alex grimaced. "I hate thinking that he could in any way have anything to do with this, but the fact that he's never been with us when you've received a phone call from Bob, the fact that he has a tendency to disappear by himself for long periods of time makes me wonder."

"Maybe you should look at his personnel file, find out what's in his background," she suggested. As somebody who had been so private about her own past, she felt bad even suggesting it.

The grimace turned into a frown. "You know a case is bad when you start looking askew at your own team members."

"You know you won't be satisfied until you check him out," she replied. "You know as well as I do, you never know what package evil comes in. Who is to say it doesn't come in the package of an overly ambitious FBI agent who committed the crime and now is determined to somehow solve the crime on his own, gaining glory and respect among the ranks."

"You're right, I won't be satisfied until he's vetted. I'll check in with Director Miller first thing in the morning and see what I can do without it coming to Nicholas's attention. And now let's talk about something else because otherwise I'm going to lose my appetite before I finish my bacon."

"That will never happen," she said teasingly.

"Probably not," he agreed with a wry grin.

They finished the meal, talking about the weather, which was predicted to cool off a little bit in the next week, and what else Georgina had learned from reading Michelle's book. After cleanup, they each carried a fresh cup of coffee into the living room and the case was once again the topic of conversation.

"It's too bad we couldn't confirm alibis on either Roger or Jax during the time I was fighting with Bob on the front lawn," she said as she eased down on one end of the sofa.

"It's too bad we only have two names on our persons of interest list—three if we count Michelle." Alex sank down on the opposite end of the sofa.

"I feel like we're missing something, but I can't figure out what it might be," she admitted. "I've read over all the files a dozen times and I can't find anything that the initial investigators missed."

"I've seen plenty of terrible things in my job, but I can't wrap my mind around somebody who would kidnap FBI agents in order to pick their brains on how to become the best serial killer in the world."

Alex shook his head and picked up his cup from the coffee table. He held the cup before him as his eyes bored into hers with intensity. "We have to get this guy, Georgina. We have to get him before he kills those people."

She saw the torment in the depths of his blue eyes, knew that he had to be thinking about the loss of Kelly Gilmer under his lead.

"We're going to get him, Alex." She couldn't help herself. She leaned over and placed her hand on his arm in an effort to ease some of his torture. "You have to let her go. You have to know that you did all that was humanly possible to save her."

The haunting in his eyes eased somewhat. "You know, when I have one of my nightmares about her, I still reach out for you in the bed. Even after all this time, in my sleep-muddied mind I'm always surprised to find that space next to me empty."

His words caused an ache in her heart, even as she pulled her hand away from him and moved closer to the edge of the sofa. She couldn't be pulled in by his needs, his wants, because ultimately she'd never live up to his expectations.

"I'm sorry, Alex. I'm sorry you're still having nightmares and that you have to go through them alone.

Maybe you should talk to somebody professionally about that case, somebody who could help you find the closure that you deserve."

"I don't need a damn shrink," he scoffed. He downed his coffee and stood. "I think I'm going to call it a night. I'll make sure the alarm is set. Just turn off the lights when you go to bed."

He didn't even bother to take his cup into the kitchen but rather headed straight down the hallway to his bedroom. She'd made him mad.

She wasn't sure what he had expected of her. If he'd expected her to volunteer to sleep in his bed with him so that she'd always be there when he had one of his nightmares, he was delusional.

As she sipped her coffee, she decided it was good that he was angry with her, that surely the conversation and her lack of a response would solidify the fact that she was not coming back to him.

She was only here now because she knew she was marked by a killer. She was only here because she trusted Alex to do everything in his power to make sure she stayed safe.

She wasn't here to hold him after he suffered from a bad dream. She wasn't here to jump back into his bed for more amazing sex or to become a partner in life once again.

Once this case was over and Bob was behind bars, things would go back to the way they had been for the past two years. She'd see Alex in passing in the building, they might exchange a few words in greeting, but that would be it.

What she didn't understand as she picked up their

cups and carried them into the kitchen was why her heart ached so badly at the thought of leaving him once again.

ALEXANDER WAS IN A FOUL MOOD. He'd been in a foul mood all morning. He'd barely spoken to Georgina as they'd shared coffee and then ridden to work together.

It wasn't so much that he was angry with her. He was angry with himself for wanting her, for needing her when she'd made it clear she was done. And maybe he'd always retained a little bit of anger toward her because she'd walked away from him so easily, without any real explanation.

His mood hadn't improved when they got to work and he'd gone in to Director Miller's office to discuss Nicholas Cutter with him. Miller had been surprised by Alexander's request to see Nicholas's personnel file, but had agreed to provide it to Alexander before the end of the day.

The mood in the war room seemed to reflect Alex's. Everyone appeared to be in a bad mood, sniping at each other when anyone spoke.

He'd finally sent several of the men home for the day, knowing that working seven days a week and the long daily hours were probably part of the problem.

When he was done, it was just himself, Georgina, Nicholas, Tim and Terry left in the room. He'd tried to send Tim home, but the young agent had refused, telling Alex he had nothing waiting for him at home and would much rather keep working on locations to search.

Georgina sat with her laptop open in front of her and her cell phone by its side. When she'd first begun work, she'd gone to Michelle Davison's web page and had discovered that the author was now using the disappearance of the three FBI agents for publicity, a fact that had put a star next to Jax's name on the whiteboard.

She was now surfing the web to find out any minute information about Jax White that she could find, but Alexander noticed how often her gaze fell on her cell phone.

Waiting for a call from Bob—that's what she was hoping for. Alexander's stomach tightened as he thought of how shattered she'd been with the last phone call. Could she handle another one? Was Bob done talking and instead now plotting on a new way to get her in one of his cages?

And what the hell had little Macy meant by saying they were in cages? He got up from his chair and began to pace the length of the room, his thoughts whirling with suppositions.

"Tim, check for old prison or jails," he said to the redheaded agent. "Macy said they were in cages. Maybe that in itself is a clue that they're being held in some old prison facility that was abandoned years ago."

"I'm on it," Tim replied, not looking up from his computer screen.

Alexander continued to pace, trying to separate Georgina's emotional turmoil from the nervous energy that filled him when he focused on the case.

He stood back and stared at the bulletin board with all the photos tacked up and staring back at him. He darted his gaze to the whiteboard, where the names of Michelle, Jax and Roger were written, along with notes about each one.

His eyes felt gritty. Despite storming off to bed fairly early, he'd been awake for most of the night. He'd tossed and turned, stared up at the ceiling and thought about what Georgina had said about him needing to let go of the Gilmer case.

On some level he recognized that he'd done everything humanly possible to save Kelly from the monster that had abducted her and then ultimately killed her. He just wished he'd been one minute sooner arriving at that warehouse, he wished he'd been able to shoot the bastard before he'd plunged that knife downward.

Maybe he did need some therapy. He'd been encouraged to see the agency shrink right after it had all happened, but he'd refused, afraid to show any weakness, afraid to admit how deeply that case had touched him.

He finally found himself back in his chair. Remembering what Georgina had told him about being a scapegoat child, he typed in the term to bring up some sites that had information on the issue.

He'd heard the term before but wasn't sure exactly what it meant. As he read first one article and then another detailing both what a scapegoat child would suffer and the lasting effects that could occur, any anger he might have felt toward Georgina slowly melted away.

If what he'd read was true, then Georgina had spent the first sixteen years of her life being told she was defective, not wanted and not loved. Her mother hadn't rushed to save her, her sisters hadn't tried to protect her; rather, the entire family had deemed her unworthy and punished her for the simple fact that she'd been born a girl.

Was it any wonder she had been guarded throughout

their marriage? Was it any wonder she'd been afraid to share the very core of her being with him? Maybe she needed therapy as much as he did.

It was close to noon when Director Miller came into the room with a file. Alex took it from him and buried it beneath his other files, knowing this one would contain the information he needed to know about Nicholas.

He'd look at it later, at home tonight, when Nicholas wasn't around. "Why don't we break for lunch," he said. "Let's plan to be back here in about an hour."

Terry, Tim and Nicholas were the first out of the room. Georgina stood and started for the door, but he stopped her. "I want to apologize for my crappy mood last night and this morning," he said.

"It's okay," she replied.

"No, it isn't okay." He took two steps closer to her, stepping into the achingly familiar scent that emanated from her. "I'm frustrated with the case, and I took it out on you." While that wasn't the complete truth, it was all he intended to say.

He couldn't tell her that he loved her, that he'd never stopped loving her. He couldn't tell her that she was an ache in his heart that was relentless. He didn't want to burden her with his problem, and it was his problem.

"What did Director Miller give you?"

"Nicholas's personnel file. We can take a look at it tonight when we get back to my place." He intentionally didn't say *home,* for *home* implied a place where they would live together, love each other.

"I still can't imagine…" Whatever else she might have said was cut off by the ring of her cell phone. Her face paled and her eyes darkened as she sat back in her chair and answered.

Alexander moved to stand right behind her as Bob's voice filled the line. "I nearly got you the other night," he said. "I decided to shake things up a bit."

"You definitely shook me up," Georgina replied, her voice strong and showing her control.

Bob laughed, the altered sound a creepy one that Alexander knew would stay in both his and Georgina's heads for a very long time to come. "You're a feisty one, Georgina, but I would have had you if your friend hadn't come along when he did. You are one lucky lady."

"Bob, why don't you end this all now? Nobody is dead and we can work together to get you help. You know we both share a similar background and I understand the rage that is driving you, but this isn't the way to heal from it. You deserve better than this."

"Oh, is this another attempt to bond with me? To find the innocent little child inside me and heal my boo-boos?" Bob's voice held derision. "How have your childhood boo-boos healed, Georgina? Have you found your inner child and fixed what your family did to you?"

Alexander saw the faint tremble of Georgina's hand as she quickly swiped it through her short hair and he knew that she hadn't resolved the issues from her past, that they still haunted her despite the fact that she was now not only an adult, but a well-respected FBI agent as well.

"You're a smart man, Bob. You didn't have to kidnap all those people to learn how to kill. You could have read all the books on crime. You could have researched and gotten the same results."

"I've done extensive research into the subject of serial killers and what drives them. I've studied case histories to understand what mistakes they made that ultimately landed them behind bars. But I also know there is a time when the teacher has to become the student and I could learn all kinds of things that weren't in books by interrogating the men who had been in the trenches."

"Then why do you need me? You have the best of the best at your disposal."

"I don't *need* you, Georgina. I just want you, and I always get what I want." There was a click and the call ended.

"Not this time," Alexander muttered under his breath.

Georgina leaned back in her chair and released a tremulous sigh. "Did you get anything out of that?"

Alexander sat next to her. "Play the recorded version."

He was grateful that she'd stayed strong and Bob hadn't played the mind games with her as he had before.

They listened to the conversation three times. There didn't appear to be any background noise and his voice held no trace of any specific characteristic that would make anything about him easily identifiable.

"There's something he said that shot off a little bell in my head," she said.

"What's that?"

"Something about it being time for the teacher to become the student." She frowned thoughtfully. "The first thing that jumped into my head was Professor Tanner."

Alexander sat back in his chair in surprise. "Professor Tanner?"

She shook her head and released a small laugh. "I know, crazy, right? Why would a highly esteemed college professor be kidnapping FBI agents to become a world-class serial killer?"

"As crazy as suspecting one of my own team having something to do with the kidnappings," he replied.

"Maybe this case has just made us both so desperate that we really are crazy and grasping at very thin straws," she said.

"Let's go down to the cafeteria and talk about what it feels like to be crazy."

"Sounds like a plan," she agreed.

As they headed out of the room, Alexander mulled over her new potential suspect and the fact that once again Nicholas hadn't been around when a call had come in. Was it possible that one of their own was responsible?

Could they really take a single line of conversation and make it point to an entirely new suspect? Or were they both grasping empty air in an effort to stop a madman?

Chapter Eleven

"Baker's Bayou," Tim said, breaking the silence that had prevailed in the war room since they'd all come back from lunch.

"What about it?" Georgina asked before Alex got the chance. The phone call with Bob followed by lunch in the cafeteria had filled her with a restless energy that refused to subside.

"In the early 1950s there was a small women's prison located there." Tim looked up from the computer screen. "It's been abandoned all these years, but it would probably still have jail cells in there."

Alex was up and out of his chair at the same time Georgina stood. "Tim, get me the exact coordinates. Nicholas, get on the phone and have Jesse Calder from Fish and Wildlife meet us there. He knows the swamps as well as anyone.

"Terry, call Matt and Frank and have them meet us at the mouth of Baker's Bayou. Get the directions from Tim and tell them to come in quiet."

Tim printed out a map with directions. Alex grabbed it and the three of them flew out the door. Georgina's heart pounded loudly in her ears as adrenaline pumped through her.

Was it possible this was it? An old abandoned jail in the middle of a swamp would certainly fit the bill for good old Bob. Was it really possible that they'd located his lair?

They didn't bother waiting for the elevator but instead took the stairs two at a time. They burst out of the back door of the building and raced to Alex's car. Terry rode shotgun and Georgina climbed into the backseat. She barely had her door closed when Alex started the car and squealed out of the parking lot.

Terry read the directions that Tim had provided and other than that there was no conversation in the car. The energy level that filled the car made it feel as if there were twenty people in the vehicle.

She didn't know the Baker's Bayou area at all, but she had worked with Jesse Calder on a case once in the past. She swore he was part man, part swamp creature and he could guide them wherever they needed to go through any swamp in the state.

She knew they were headed into danger. Anytime there was a possibility of a hostage situation, everyone's lives were at risk, particularly the hostages themselves.

The best they could all hope for was that when they did their initial preview of the building, Bob wouldn't be there. She didn't believe that Bob spent all of his time with his hostages. He had to have a job; if nothing else he had to make money to feed the people he held captive.

Sam and Daniella and little Macy had been missing for months. If they weren't being fed, they would have already starved to death.

She glanced down at her watch. It was just after four. If they were lucky, they'd have at least four hours of daylight to maneuver and get into the place Tim had found. Darkness came early in the swamp and even with Jesse's guidance, night would complicate the whole operation.

Her adrenaline shot higher when Alex told Terry to contact the rest of the team. He obviously thought that this was the break they'd been waiting for and they were on their way to save the people who had been missing for too long.

If they were really lucky, they could get into the building and wait for Bob to arrive. That way they would not only ensure the safety of the hostages, but get him under arrest at the same time.

She wanted that. She wanted the man who had caused such chaos, such pain, to be behind bars for the rest of his life where he couldn't hurt anyone else ever again.

It felt as if it took forever to reach the location, but finally they were there and Alex parked on the grass near a dirt road that led into what she assumed was Baker's Bayou.

When they got out of the car, the smell of the swamp hung in the air. The odor was fishy and one of stinking stagnant water and thick sucking mud.

The dirt road disappeared into a heavily wooded area, where cypress trees were nearly overwhelmed by Spanish moss, giving the whole area a spooky aura.

Georgina fought back a shiver as she stared into the semidarkness of the marsh. There was haunting beauty there, but there was also danger…and potentially seven people who desperately needed to be rescued.

She touched the butt of her holstered gun that was on

a belt around her waist. She'd never had to kill a man before, but she wouldn't hesitate to put a bullet into Bob's black heart if it became necessary.

Her firm resolve came from the memory of Macy's frightened voice, the little girl's blue eyes that looked at her day after day from her photo in the war room.

The nearby swamp wasn't silent. Mosquitoes buzzed in the air, brush rustled and in the distance a watery slap indicated either a big fish or a gator.

"We'll wait here until Jesse and the others arrive," Alex said, his deep voice filled with tension. "According to this map that Tim printed out, there's only one way in and one way out of Baker's Bayou." He pointed to the dirt road.

"Are there any homes in the area?" Terry asked.

"There might be a couple, but they look like they're pretty close to the mouth. The building we're looking at is toward the back of the cove. I just hope we don't need a boat to get back there."

"Surely Jesse will know, and if we need a boat he'll have one with him," Georgina replied.

They all turned as two cars arrived, one carrying Matt and Frank and the other with Nicholas behind the wheel and Jeff in the passenger seat. The men got out and Alex quickly filled them in.

"When Jesse arrives, Frank, Matt and I will go in with him. Terry, Nicholas, Jeff and Georgina will stand guard here to make sure that nobody comes out this way."

"I'm not staying here," Georgina said firmly. "I'm going in with you."

"Georgina, you're a target. I don't want you anyplace

near this man." Alex's eyes simmered with emotion as he attempted to stare her down.

She stared right back at him, her chin lifted in a show of resolve. She hadn't come this far, suffered this much, to be relegated to the back of the line. She deserved to go in.

"I'm a trained FBI agent and I'm the only person here who has a personal relationship with Bob. I might be your only hope if things go bad. I'm coming with you."

His eyes narrowed to blue slits of displeasure, even as he gave a curt nod of his head. "Okay, but you'll be sandwiched between me and Jesse as we go in."

"Whatever, as long as I go in with you," she replied, pleased that he had listened to her, even though it was obvious he hadn't wanted to.

Nobody was going to keep her out. She wanted to be there when the hostages were freed. She also wanted to be there if things went bad and somebody had to negotiate with Bob.

Jesse pulled up in a black pickup. He got out and strode toward them, looking like he was already part of the swamp. He wore a long-sleeved camouflage shirt and pants that disappeared into hip waders.

His long black hair was tied at the nape of his neck and his dark eyes were as flat as the gators he knew so well. He greeted them all with a raise of his hand and then took the map Matt proffered and studied it.

"I know this place," he said. "Been back there a couple of times over the years. We won't need a boat. There's a narrow muddy path of sorts that we can walk with water on either side. The water is fairly deep and full of gators and snapping turtles and other critters. I suggest you all step where I step if you want to be as safe as possible."

"We want to go in quiet and see if we can get a look inside," Alex replied. "We don't know if the man we're hunting is there or not."

Jesse's eyes gleamed with excitement. "Then let the hunt begin." Without another word he headed toward the dirt road. Georgina hurried after him with Alex and Frank and Matt bringing up the rear.

They walked in single file down the road and within minutes reached an old shanty. Jesse and Georgina stood back as Matt and Alex checked out the place.

"It's obviously been abandoned for years," Alex said as he emerged from the listing structure. He motioned for them to forge ahead.

The road continued for about half a mile and then narrowed to a path and the swamp took over. Tall cypress, oak and elm trees blocked out much of the light of the day, the oaks wearing Spanish moss like delicate hair.

Georgina followed in Jesse's footsteps but began to feel the suck of muck on her feet. The swampy smell was more intense and the bugs thicker and bigger. Pools of water stood on either side of the narrow path. Georgina kept her gaze focused on the path. She didn't want to see what creatures the waters might hold.

If this was the right place, then how on earth had Bob managed to get the hostages through here? "Is there a waterway to the building where we're going?" she asked Jesse, keeping her voice as soft as possible.

"Yeah, you could get there by a pirogue, you'd just have to enter the area north of where we did," Jesse replied.

Georgina knew that a pirogue was a canoe-like boat and she also knew that the boats could be big enough to carry a body or two. Unfortunately, these boats weren't registered through the state so there was no way of finding Bob by his means of transportation through the swampland, if that's the way he traveled.

With each step she took, she felt the muck beneath her feet suck harder, making the simple act of walking difficult. Her shoes and pants would be ruined, but that was a tiny sacrifice to make if they were successful in freeing the victims and catching Bob.

The primal wildness that surrounded her added to the tension of the situation. The deeper they went into the marsh, the faster her heart beat, and a thin layer of perspiration began to coat her forehead.

They'd all pulled their guns when they'd begun the trek, and hers now felt slippery in her hand as the sultry heat made sweat trickle down her back and streak from her hair.

Get Bob. Free the captives. The two sentences became her mantra as they continued to walk for what felt like forever. Get Bob. Free the captives.

Would Bob turn out to be Jax or Roger or would he be somebody they hadn't even met, somebody who hadn't hit their radar?

Just when Georgina thought she couldn't lift her mud-caked feet for another step, Jesse stopped and turned back to face them.

"The building is just ahead. It's on dry ground. I

don't know how you want to handle the approach," he said. "I could go ahead and check it out, see if the people you're looking for are there."

Alex frowned. "I appreciate the offer, but you've done your job by getting us here. I'd like it if you'd wait here to get us back out, but trained agents need to be the ones making contact from here."

Adrenaline flooded through her and she forgot about the muck, the sweat and the bugs as she realized they were within sight of the place that hopefully would end this case once and for all.

"Matt and Frank, you go to the left of the building and Georgina and I will go right. Try to get close enough to look inside without being seen by anyone. We don't want a hostage situation. We go in slow and quiet." Alex's terse voice spoke of the danger in the situation.

"And if they're in there and Bob isn't anywhere to be seen?"

"There has to be a front door of some kind. We'll see what we can see and then if that's the case we'll meet at the front door to go in as a team." He looked at Georgina. "Ready?"

She nodded. She'd never been more ready for anything in her life. Her head filled with the sound of Macy's voice asking for help. "Let's get this done."

The four of them moved ahead where the path widened and although the area was heavily treed, the land rose higher than the swamp waters that surrounded it.

Through the thick stand of trees and brush, she could see the structure, a rather small, concrete-block building. Small windows were set high at regularly spaced intervals, each sporting a rusty-looking set of bars.

The place looked utterly abandoned, as if the swamp and the primordial wilderness had tried to swallow it whole. This was a place where people could scream and nobody would hear. This was a place that only a swamp rat would know about. And they'd already discerned that Bob was probably a spawn of the swamp.

As the two pairs split up, Georgina's heart banged painfully tight against her ribs as the first tinge of hope she'd felt since beginning this case filled her. The emotion pressed tight in her chest, making her feel almost dizzy with anticipation.

They made their way stealthily through the brush and around the trees toward the right side of the building. Hopefully there would be a window somewhere on the side or in the back that would allow them to see inside without actually breaching the building.

Let them be here, Georgina thought as she stayed close to Alex. Bugs bit at her and branches slapped her arms and legs as they worked through the woods and tried to stay covered from view.

Her heartbeat raced even faster as they finally reached the side of the building and saw a door with a window. Alex exchanged glances with her and in his eyes she saw the same hope that jumped inside her very soul.

Seeing nobody around and using the brush and trees to their advantage, they moved forward. Georgina got to the door first and carefully raised her head just enough to peek inside.

Her heart dropped to the muddy ground beneath her. Empty. Abandoned. There was nobody inside to save and it appeared that nobody had been inside the structure for years and years.

Alex muttered a curse as she turned and leaned against him, overwhelmed by the sense of defeat, of knowing that they were no closer to catching Bob and saving the victims than they'd been on the very first day that the task force had been formed.

Wearily she straightened and headed back. Failure. The weight of it was an accustomed one, a reminder that she would never be good enough, had never been good enough for much of anything.

Failure. It was the first thing she'd tasted when she'd been old enough to understand that she wasn't what her family wanted, and she hated that the taste was no different now.

IT WAS AFTER SEVEN when Alexander left the FBI building with Georgina at his side. The disappointment that the entire team had suffered when they'd arrived back at the war room was palpable.

He'd been so sure. He'd been so positive that they'd found the place where the captives were just waiting to be released from their cages.

As he drove home, all he heard was the loud ticking of a clock in his head, an instinctive clock that told him time was quickly running out for Bob's hostages.

Seeing the location of the old jail, recognizing how many other places there could be in the back of any number of swamps, had shot a wave of discouragement through him that he hadn't been able to shake no matter how hard he tried.

He pulled into the driveway and together they got

out of the car and went into the house. "Dinner?" She looked at him in question, her gaze holding a dull light of defeat.

"I'm not really hungry. What I'd like is a nice stiff drink."

"I'm of a mind to join you," she replied as she sat at the kitchen table.

Alexander opened the cabinet that held his small liquor collection. "I've got whiskey, scotch and there might even be a bottle of wine up here."

"To hell with the wine. I'll take scotch on the rocks," she said.

He looked at her with a raised brow. She normally wasn't much of a drinker, other than an occasional glass of wine. *But you don't know what she's done during the past two years,* he reminded himself. Still, she'd always been a lightweight when it came to holding her liquor.

He poured them both scotch on the rocks and then joined her at the table. Dark shadows rode the delicate skin beneath her eyes and her entire body appeared smaller, as if she'd pulled into herself. She wore the defeat of the day on her face and·in her posture.

She took a sip of the scotch and made a face. "I've never understood how people drink this stuff. I think it tastes awful."

"You want me to get you something else?"

She shook her head. "No, tonight I need something strong and biting." She released a weary sigh. "I was so sure we were right, Alex. I was so certain that we were at the end of the case and everything was going to be good. We were going to rescue everyone and get the bad guy behind bars."

"I know. I felt the same way. Seeing that empty, abandoned building kicked the stuffing out of my gut." He downed his scotch in two swallows and then got up from the table, grabbed the bottle and returned. He poured himself another two fingers of the amber liquid.

Georgina tipped up her glass and downed her drink, then gestured for him to refill her glass as well. He did so and then leaned back in his chair, a deep weariness settling heavily on his shoulders, into his very soul.

"You have to promise me something, Alex," she said, her green eyes the color of the swamp that had earlier surrounded them.

"Promise what?" he asked.

"Promise me that if this all goes bad, you won't go back to that dark place where you went with the Gilmer case."

He turned his glass around and around between his hands as he stared down into the scotch. "There's only been one thing that took me back to that dark place, one thing that took me even deeper into the darkness, and that was you walking out on me."

He looked up at her, his heart filled with the love he feared he'd always hold where she was concerned. "I thought the Gilmer darkness was bad, but the pit of darkness I fell into when you left me was even worse."

She broke eye contact with him and instead leaned back in her chair and released a deep sigh. "I thought it was the best thing to do for you."

She took another drink and he couldn't help but notice that her cheeks had filled with pink spots of color, a sign that she was feeling the effects of the alcohol.

When they'd been married he'd always known when

she was getting tipsy by the blushing red that saturated her cheeks. Apparently she was still a lightweight when it came to alcohol.

Maybe now was the time to have the conversation they'd never had, the one where she told him exactly what had driven her away from him.

"You know what I hate most about Bob? I hate him because he got pieces of your past, he got your tears, he got from you things I never got from you."

"I told you before, that was something I didn't want to drag into the marriage with you." She took another sip of her scotch despite the fact that her voice already had a small slur. "Things were so good with us, I didn't want you to know the ugliness of my past. I only told Bob about those things in an effort to help the case."

"I did a little research this morning on scapegoat child syndrome," he confessed.

She took another drink and then pushed her glass away. "Then you know the gist of what my childhood was like. Basically it stank." She reached up and stroked her fingers through her short hair and cast him a slightly bitter, rueful smile. "When I was fourteen I had hair down below my shoulders. As a last-ditch effort to be what my father wanted me to be, I cut it all off."

She released a burst of laughter that was laced with pain, the pain she'd never shared with him. The pain he would do anything to assuage if only she'd allow him in. "Of course it didn't work," she continued. "I was the child who should have never been born and my family never let me forget it."

He wanted to hold her. He wanted to cradle her close and tell her how precious she was, what an amazing person she was despite her tragic beginnings, but she sat rigid in her chair, her chin uplifted in a defensive mode that kept him in his seat across from her.

"You understand that it was never about you, that it was your parents who were dysfunctional."

"Thank you, Dr. Harkins," she replied lightly, but with a faint hint of sarcasm. "Rationally I know that now. When I went into foster care I was told that again and again. The scars I carry are deep, but they're old scars."

"I don't think those scars are as healed over as you tell yourself they are," he replied. He also shoved his glass away. He didn't want to be tipsy to have this conversation with her. He wanted to be clearheaded with all his faculties intact when he asked her what had eaten at him for the last two years.

"Why did you leave me, Georgina? Why wasn't I enough for you? What could I have done differently to make you feel safe and secure enough to share it all with me? Why couldn't I make you feel completely loved and not afraid to give love back?"

"Oh, Alex, the problem was never you. It's always been about me. It always will be me." Her eyes grew misty as she held his gaze. "You're right. Some of the scars aren't as healed as I want them to be. I thought I could be normal. When I fell in love with you, I thought I could get married and have children and walk away from my childhood whole. But the truth of the matter is that I'm damaged goods, Alex. You deserve better and far more than what I could ever give to you."

"You're wrong, Georgina. You were always all that I ever wanted, and you didn't give me enough credit if you believed I couldn't handle both the best and the very worst of you." He leaned forward, his heart aching with all the emotions that had assailed him since the moment she'd left their marriage.

She closed her eyes, as if to shut out whatever else he wanted to say. "It was the right thing for me to do," she repeated. "I only wanted what was best for you, and that wasn't me. That could never be me."

"Did you love me when you left me?" His heart hurt so much. "Georgina, open your eyes and look at me. I need to see your beautiful eyes when you answer me," he said.

She opened her eyes and their green depths were filled with such pain. "Yes, I loved you when I left. I left *because* I loved you so much." Once again she threaded her fingers through her rich, dark hair.

"When you were dealing with the aftermath of the Gilmer case, having bad dreams and so obviously in pain, I didn't know what to say to you. I didn't have the words to comfort you." A single tear fell from each of her eyes and splashed down on her pink cheeks. "I knew then that I couldn't be, would never be, enough for you."

Alexander couldn't stand it any longer. He needed to touch her, to hold her. He got up from his chair and walked around the table to where she sat. As he touched her arm, she folded into herself, as if protecting herself from any onslaught that might hurt.

"Georgina," he whispered her name softly. Tears chased faster down her cheeks. "Honey, all you had to do for me was just be there. When I had my nightmares and I turned over in the bed, you were always there to hold me. I didn't need words from you. I just needed to know that you were next to me. That was enough. You were enough."

He pulled on her arm and breathed a ragged sigh of relief when she unfolded, rose and fell into his embrace. She began to cry and he savored each of her tears, knowing they were a form of cathartic release she rarely allowed herself.

She leaned weakly against him as he stroked his hands up and down her back. He relished her weakness as it was a gift she'd never given to him before. It was a sign that she trusted him enough to give him her tears.

He knew it wouldn't last long, that she would quickly pull herself together and be the strong, stubborn, independent woman she'd always been. But for now, he just wanted to hold her while she dealt with her pain.

"I never stopped loving you, Georgina," he said softly. "I tried to stop. I didn't want to keep loving you, but I couldn't help it. I'd see you in the hallway at work and it would be like an arrow piercing through my heart. There hasn't been a day since our divorce that I haven't wanted you back in this house, back in my life."

She'd stopped crying, but she didn't move from his arms. He relished the feel of her so close against him, her heart beating rapidly against his own. This was where she belonged...in his arms forever.

"Come back to me, Georgina. Come back and be my wife, my lover, my life partner. Nothing has been good since you left me." He was baring his very soul to her, feeling more vulnerable than he'd ever felt in his life.

She raised her head to look up at him, her eyes simmering with emotion. "Alex, I..."

Whatever she was about to say was interrupted by

a loud knock on the front door. They both froze and stepped apart.

Alexander looked at his watch. It was almost ten. Who would be at his door at this time of night?

"I'll be right back," he said to her. "We aren't finished here, Georgina."

She released a sigh and nodded.

As he walked to the door, he pulled his gun, unsure what or who to expect. It might be one of the team members dropping by with new information or it could be something else altogether.

He looked out the peephole, and when he saw who was there, a shock of surprise swept through him. He holstered his gun and opened the door. "Hey, what's going on?" He stepped out on the porch.

Before he could speak another word, he felt a sharp sting in his upper back. He reached an arm up and felt the dart that still clung to his body.

At the same time, a weakness attacked his muscles. He tried to remain upright, but his legs had turned to jelly and his brain felt wrapped in cotton.

Trouble. Georgina was in danger.

This was his final thought as he fell to the ground next to the stoop and the last of his consciousness slipped away.

Chapter Twelve

"Alex?" Georgina called from the kitchen when he didn't immediately return. Who could he be talking to for so long and why hadn't they come inside?

"Alex, is everything okay?" She left the kitchen and her breath hitched in her chest as she met a masked man in the living room. Before she could draw her gun, a dart struck her in the chest.

She stared down at it in disbelief at the same time she fumbled to get her gun from the holster. But nothing was working right. Her legs were going out from under her, and even when her hand finally landed on the butt of her gun, she didn't have the strength to pull the weapon.

She tried to speak, but her mouth wouldn't form the words of panic, the scream of terror that was trapped inside her. He merely stood before her, his face hidden but blue eyes gleaming from the holes in the mask.

"Just let go, Georgina. Give in to it. You can't fight the drugs."

His voice sounded vaguely familiar, but her brain refused to recognize it as darkness began to creep into her head, a darkness that finally pulled her under and she knew no more.

She dreamed that she was a child and once again her father had locked her in the closet because she was a bad girl. She wasn't sure what she'd done wrong to receive the punishment. He'd just looked at her and gotten angry.

She never knew how long she'd be locked up and hated the weekends when it was possible she'd spend all of Saturday and Sunday inside the small, dark enclosure. Her sisters knocked on the door and called her names and laughed, deepening the pain of the isolation.

No good, piece of dirt, a waste of space and oxygen, over and over again their voices called to her, telling her just how bad she was and how they wished she'd never been born.

Then she was a grown-up and Alex was by her side. Alex. Someplace in the blackness of her drug-induced sleep, her heart cried out to him.

Was he dead or alive? It was a nebulous question that floated around in her head, but she couldn't hang onto the thought as other visions and nightmares returned to visit her.

She had no idea how long she'd been unconscious when she began to wake up. She was on a thin mattress, but for several minutes she didn't open her eyes; rather, she listened to the sounds around her.

Whispers.

Was she still a little girl? Were the whispers those of her sisters making fun of her again? No, that wasn't right. She wasn't a child anymore, and as she remembered encountering the masked man in Alex's living room, she knew what had happened.

Bob had gotten her into his lair.

She opened her eyes and found herself on a lower bunk bed in a jail-like cell. She didn't move, but rather allowed her gaze to take in all the details of her surroundings.

There was a sink, a toilet and a shower nozzle and a curtain hanging down that could be pulled around the toilet and shower to provide some modicum of privacy.

She closed her eyes once again, her heart pounding with fear and her head aching with the residual effects of whatever drug Bob had shot her with.

Why would Alex open the door to a man wearing a ski mask? And what had happened to Alex? Had he merely been drugged and left behind, or had Bob killed him?

No, Alex couldn't be dead. She absolutely, positively refused to believe that. He had to live and he had to find her. But how could he? How could the task force find her when they had no leads, no clues to follow?

Blue eyes. That's all she remembered. Did Jax White have blue eyes? Did Roger? God help her, she couldn't remember.

"Georgina, are you awake?"

It was Jackson's soft, drawling voice. She turned on her side and opened her eyes once again, now able to see that Jackson and a pretty strawberry-blonde woman were in the next cell. And beyond their cell she could see the others.

"I'm awake, but I have the headache from hell," she replied.

"It's whatever drug he used. It will go away pretty quickly," he replied. "You might have a bit of amnesia, as well. Some of us suffered from a lack of memories concerning our kidnapping for a couple of days. Must be a side effect of the drug."

Georgina nodded, although she didn't think she had any amnesia.

"You must be Marjorie," Georgina said to the woman. "Alex told me all about you."

"So Alexander is working the case?" Jackson asked eagerly.

Georgina pulled herself to a sitting position, careful not to hit her aching head on the top bunk. "There's a task force working on finding you all." She realized everyone in the room was listening to her. "Do you know who your captor is?"

"No, so far he's always worn a ski mask when he comes in here," Jackson replied. "The task force…do they have any clues? Are they getting close to finding us?"

Georgina heard the hope in Jackson's voice and she didn't have the heart to completely crush it. "We had several people of interest we were looking at. I'm sure it won't be too long now before they narrow it down. The police department is also helping to check out old buildings where we hoped to find that you all were being held."

"And yet he managed to get you." Sam Connelly's voice came from the distance, although his "cell" was too far away for her to see him.

"Georgina, I talked to you on the phone. Remember me? I'm Macy." The childish voice sliced through Georgina's heart.

"I remember, honey," she replied. "And it won't be long now before we're all out of here."

Jackson moved closer to the bars that separated them. With effort, Georgina got up from the bed and joined him. He reached his fingers through and she covered them with her own.

"How close are they really to finding us?" he asked, his voice once again a low whisper.

She hesitated and realized he wanted the truth, not some fairy tale to keep everyone filled with false hope. "Not close at all. The task force is working every angle and hopefully they'll figure it all out."

"How did he get to you?"

"I was staying with Alex. There was a knock on the door. Alex answered, and when he didn't come back to the kitchen, I walked into the living room and encountered the perp."

"And he got you with a dart," Jackson said flatly. "That's how he got us all. So exactly what's being done?"

For the next few minutes she filled him in on the task force investigation, the connection they all had with Michelle Davison's book and the fact that Roger had been at all of the crime scenes.

"We know he grew up in the swamp and according to him he killed his mother and father. We believe he has some level of higher education and that he's obsessed with becoming the perfect, unstoppable serial killer."

"I think it's a good sign for us that he hasn't shown us his identity," Jackson said. "Once we see his face, once we all know what he looks like, there's no way he'll allow us to walk out of here free and clear. He carries a gun and eventually he'll use it to kill us. To be honest, I think that time is growing near. Over the last couple of days he seems to have lost interest in whatever he thinks he can learn from us. He feeds us but then leaves, and there's a new restlessness in him that feels dangerous."

Jackson moved away from the bars and placed an arm around Marjorie and they both sat in the bottom bunk as Georgina returned to her own bunk.

Once again she lay down on her back and stared up at the bottom of the upper bunk. Was Alex alive? She could only assume that he'd been hit with a dart. Was he conscious? Were he and the team now hunting, frantic to find them before time ran out? Or had the dart that had pierced him held enough of the drug to be lethal?

One thing was certain. Nobody was going to die until Bob got a chance to talk to her, to crow about the fact that he'd once again managed to kidnap an FBI agent and get her into this hellhole. He'd want to brag about taking her from right under the protection of Alex.

She closed her eyes again, aware of the other couples talking quietly among themselves. A vision of Alex filled her head as she replayed the conversation they'd been having before being interrupted.

She couldn't think about it. She couldn't deal with it right now. She just had to pray that Alex was still alive and the task force was tearing up every street and building in the entire city.

He feeds us but then leaves. Jackson's words reverberated around in her head, along with a horrifying thought. Bob wouldn't have to use his gun or his darts to kill any of them. All he would have to do is stop coming, stop feeding them and they would all die a slow and painful death.

ALEX WOKE UP to the scent of grass and a headache that made his stomach roll with nausea. He remained immobile for several minutes, his brain too fogged to think.

He finally turned over and realized he was outside of his house on the lawn, his front door wide open as if to invite in any nefarious creatures. Snakes could slither in, a wandering gator could go inside, or Bob could make an unexpected appearance.

Bob!

A rush of thoughts frantically worked through his mind as he struggled to get to his feet. Georgina! Her name scalded his brain as he forced his legs into action. Even as he flew through the front door, he knew she wasn't here.

Still, he raced through every room of the house, frantically calling her name, praying that she'd somehow managed to hide from danger. But he knew in his gut, he knew in his soul, she was gone.

Bob had taken her from him, and now Alexander had no idea where she was or what was happening to her. Thick emotion made it nearly impossible for him to breathe as he raced back to the front door and stared out into the night.

A glance at his watch let him know he had been unconscious for well over an hour. Bob could have taken Georgina anywhere in that length of time.

A sob of despair rose up in his throat, but he swallowed hard against it. Now wasn't the time. He needed to get the team together. They had to figure out where Bob was keeping his captives now more than ever, because now Alexander's Georgina was among the victims.

He had to shove his emotions aside. It was time to

get to work, time to figure out what they had missed and find Georgina and all the others.

It took him only minutes to make the calls that would bring the men back to the war room. As Alexander got into his car to head toward headquarters, he saw the file folder that Director Miller had given him, the folder that held Nicholas's personal information.

He took a moment with the car running to turn on the interior light and peruse the information contained in the file. As he read, a burning fire lit in the pit of his stomach.

He slammed the file down into the passenger seat and roared out of his driveway. He schooled his mind to blankness, focusing only on getting to headquarters.

He couldn't think about Georgina or what she might be suffering at this very moment. If he did that, then he'd lose his mind and be no good to anyone and she needed him to be at the top of his game.

The drive to the FBI building normally took about twenty minutes. Tonight Alexander made it in ten. He was the first one in the war room. Although his instincts all screamed for him to get outside, to rip down buildings and yell Georgina's name, he knew that kind of frantic exercise would accomplish nothing.

He made a pot of coffee and then sank down in a chair, trying to remember what exactly had happened before he'd hit the dirt in his yard.

He and Georgina had been having a talk. She'd been crying and he'd held her. He'd been telling her how he'd never stopped loving her and then there had been a knock at the door.

Frowning, he rubbed the center of his forehead. Who

had been at the door? It couldn't have been any of their persons of interest, for he would have greeted them with his gun in his hand.

The dart had struck him in the back, meaning Bob had been behind him. So who had been on his doorstep? It had to have been somebody who caused him no alarm, but he couldn't remember.

He pressed the center of his forehead, trying to retrieve a vision of who had been on his doorstep when he'd peeked outside. Who had been Bob's partner in crime?

The clue to everything was locked in his brain, and the harder he tried to remember, the more nebulous the whole event at his front door seemed.

Drugs. Maybe his missing memory was a residual effect of whatever drug Bob had used on the dart that had knocked him out cold. He looked up as Frank and Matt flew into the room.

"I need one of you to find out where Roger Cambridge has been this evening and I want the other to check on Michelle and Jax." Was it possible he'd looked outside and seen Michelle on the front porch and Jax had been lying in wait for him?

"Done," they both said in unison.

Before they could leave the room, Nicholas walked in, and before he could say a word, Alexander rushed toward him and grabbed him by the front of the shirt.

"Where have you been tonight, swamp rat?" Alexander snarled. "Why didn't you mention that you grew up in Sampson's Swamp? Why have you never been around when Bob calls Georgina?"

"Hey, what's going on?" Matt asked as he tried to get

between the two men, but Alexander wasn't letting go of Nicholas until he got some answers. "Where is she, Nicholas? Where is Georgina?"

"Do you really think I have anything to do with this?" Nicholas looked at Alexander in stunned surprise. "I've been busting my ass to solve this case and the reason I didn't mention my swamp background was because it was nothing to brag about."

Nicholas's cheeks fired a dusty red. "Let go of me. It's not a damn crime to be ashamed of where you came from. I'm not the enemy here. I'm here to help you get her back from whoever has her."

Alexander saw the truth in Nicholas's eyes and he released the man's shirt and backed away. "I read your file and saw that you were from the swamp and my head started whirling with all kinds of possibilities," he said.

Nicholas straightened his shirt and continued to look at Alexander. "I'll admit I haven't exactly been a team player, but I swear I have nothing to do with these crimes and I had nothing to do with Georgina being taken. What we need to do is figure out how to find her and the rest of them now."

Alexander stared at Nicholas hollowly. "I don't know what we need to do in order to achieve that. I'm lost."

"We aren't," Matt said and jostled Frank's shoulder. "We're going to check out where Roger, Michelle and Jax are right now and where they have been for the last couple of hours. We'll get back to you as soon as we have some answers." With that the two men left the room, passing Tim and Terry as they entered.

Alexander slumped down into a chair once again and

buried his face in his hands. He was vaguely aware of Tim firing up his computer as Terry and Nicholas sat on either side of him.

"Tell us exactly what happened," Nicholas said. "How did he get to her?"

The question created a sharp pain that sliced through Alexander. "He got to her by going through me." He raced a hand through his hair in frustration. "Somebody knocked on the door. I looked out and opened the door without my weapon drawn, but I can't remember who was on the front stoop. I stepped out and Bob blew a dart into my back."

"So we know Bob is working with an accomplice," Nicholas said. "Was it possible you'd open your door and feel no danger if you saw Michelle Davison standing there?"

"I don't know...maybe." Alexander looked at the men on either side of him and then stared at the bulletin board where Georgina's picture would soon be added.

Dammit, he felt as if the key was in his head. If he could only remember who had knocked on his door, he would know who was responsible for not just the seven victims' disappearances, but Georgina's as well.

"All I know for sure is that the end is coming fast," he continued. "He wanted Georgina and now he has her. She completes what he wanted and it won't be long before he'll be finished with all of them."

He hoped the overwhelming hopelessness he felt didn't show on his face, didn't radiate from his eyes. He had to think positive. They *would* find Bob before he could hurt any of his victims, before he could hurt Georgina.

He just needed to think and remember. Otherwise he had a feeling there would be no rescue, there would be no more Georgina.

Chapter Thirteen

"Good morning, my dear friends. And a special good morning to my newest guest, sweet Georgina."

Bob's voice was like fingernails on a chalkboard, interrupting the happy dream she'd been having about Alex. She sat up and heard the sound of the others awakening.

Morning? Where had the night gone? The last thing she remembered was staring up at the underside of the top bunk. She'd obviously fallen asleep and the night had passed, without rescue, without hope.

She stood and moved to the front of her cell as a masked Bob pushed a tray containing a breakfast sandwich and a cup of coffee through an opening at the bottom of the bars.

He straightened and his blue eyes gleamed with glee. "I'm so happy to have you here, Georgina. We have so much to talk about and it's much nicer talking in person rather than over the phone."

"I can't imagine anything we have to discuss," she replied. She grabbed the tray and took it to her bunk where she sat down with her back to him.

He laughed, obviously amused by her little show of

defiance. "Unfortunately, I have a busy day today and don't have time to visit with you this morning, but I'll be back later and we're going to have a nice chat together."

He delivered trays to each of the others, and then came back to stand in front of Georgina's cell. "I've wanted you here since the moment I first saw you and I always get what I want. You *will* talk to me later, otherwise I'll start killing the others one by one, and I'll start with the smallest."

He'd kept his voice soft, little more than a whisper, but his words shot chills up Georgina's spine until he finally left the big room.

"Bastard," Jackson hissed.

Georgina turned on her bed, careful not to upend her tray, and looked at him. Jackson had always been an incredibly handsome man, but at the moment he looked haggard, with deep stress lines cutting across his forehead and down the sides of his mouth.

"They'll find us," she said, recognizing that she was trying to reassure herself as much as him. "Alex and his team won't stop until they find us."

"Yeah, but will we all be dead by then?" Jackson asked softly. "I got the feeling from talking to you last night that the task force didn't have many clues."

Georgina took a sip of the bitter, black coffee before replying. There was no way she wanted the people here to know that the task force only had three potential persons of interest and even they were weak suspects at best.

She didn't want to take away the tiny ray of hope that still remained by telling them the team had no idea where they were being held or who was responsible for their kidnappings.

"They had clues. We felt we were getting close." The little white lie fell off her tongue without apology. Nothing could be served here by telling the truth—that the task force had been scrambling without success for answers, that they were no closer to finding out who was responsible or where the victims were than they'd been on the day the task force had been formed.

She took another drink of the coffee and looked around the space. It was a big room made of concrete blocks with the cells running along one side and nothing but a folding chair on the other side.

There were several doorways, which led her to believe there was more than this single room to the building. "Has anyone been able to figure out what this place is?" she asked.

"I think it's an old women's prison," Jackson said. "In the back of Baker's Bayou."

She shook her head. "We checked out that place yesterday." Dear God, had it only been yesterday that they had marched through the swamp, so certain that they were headed for success?

"Then that shoots my theory all to hell. But I do believe we're somewhere in a swamp. I can smell it. I can feel it. Unfortunately, I have no idea what swamp or what kind of place this might have been."

Georgina looked around her cell. "I think he must have somehow built the cells himself. If it was an old prison, there wouldn't be showers in each one or privacy curtains for the occupants. All the prisons I've ever seen have a communal shower room, not individual ones."

"He definitely planned this out for a long time. We're being fed twice a day and he's even brought clean clothes to the others a couple of times since they've been here. The overhead lights are on all the time so the only way we know it's daytime is when he brings us breakfast."

As Georgina ate her breakfast sandwich, Jackson continued to tell her about the conversations Bob had shared with each of the agents, conversations that had revolved around the mistakes serial killers made that got them caught.

Education—that's what Bob was looking for. And who better to learn from than the men and women who chased the monsters? There comes a time when the teacher has to become the student. Bob's words whirled around in her head and again the only name she thought of was Dr. Jacob Tanner, a professor who immersed himself in teaching about serial killers.

Was it possible that he had decided that teaching about them wasn't enough, that he needed action and to become what he taught about?

It didn't matter what she thought. It didn't matter if Bob was really Jacob Tanner. She couldn't give any information to Alex to help him find them. All she could do was wait…and pray that somehow, someway, he'd figure things out.

THE NIGHT HAD BEEN ENDLESS. Alexander now stood at the window, sipping a fresh cup of coffee as he watched the dawn streaking across the sky.

His eyes were gritty from lack of sleep and his heart held a hopelessness that could cast him to his knees if he allowed it. The only thing they'd learned through the night was that Roger, Michelle and Jax all had solid alibis for the time that Georgina had been taken from Alexander's house.

He leaned his head against the window glass and closed his eyes, angry that he couldn't remember who had been on his front porch…who had lured him out enough that Bob could dart him in the back and render him unconscious.

If he could just remember. He tapped the glass with his forehead in an effort to dredge up a name, a face, anything that he could hang onto. He knew that he held the key to finding Georgina and the others, but it was locked inside his brain and at the moment seemed irretrievable.

He finally turned from the window and sat at the table. He and Tim were the only ones in the war room. The others were using the light of day to recheck his house, which was now a crime scene.

They would check to make sure they hadn't missed anything in the dark of night. They also intended to canvass the neighborhood to see if anyone had seen or heard anything at the time that Georgina had been taken and he'd been drugged.

Tim had worked through the night on the computer, trying to find something, anything, that would break the case wide open. He typed with fevered fingers, as if believing that finding the location was the only way to solve the crime.

Georgina. Alexander's heart cried her name, his very soul ached with the need to find her, to save her from whatever fate Bob had in store for her and all the victims of his craziness.

He took another sip of his coffee, feeling utterly helpless, much the way he had felt during most of the Gilmer case when a young woman's fate had hung in the balance.

Now it wasn't a young woman he'd never met. It was his beloved Georgina, and he knew if something happened and she died, he would never get over it. He would crawl into the blackest hole of pain and never, ever be able to climb back out.

Agony. He was in sheer agony. The key to everything was locked in his head and refused to be dislodged. If he could only remember who had been on his front porch. Who he had felt no danger from when he'd opened his front door and had stepped out on the porch. It couldn't have been any of the potential suspects, for he would have pulled his gun before opening the door for any of them.

He closed his eyes and drew a deep sigh. Remember…he had to remember, and instantly a vision filled his head. He and Georgina had been talking about their relationship. He'd told her that he still loved her and she'd been about to reply when the knock on the door had sounded.

Suddenly a vision of the person who had been standing on his porch the night before appeared in his head. His eyes snapped open. What was her name? He not only remembered seeing her on his porch but he remembered where he had seen her before…in Dr. Jacob Tanner's office.

His heart raced as his body filled with a burst of wel-

come adrenaline that had been sadly missing throughout the darkness of the long night.

Megan. Her name was Megan. What was her last
name? He frowned and fought against an edge of excitement that sliced through him. As he replayed the
day that he and Georgina went to speak to Dr. Tanner
about Michelle, he thought about the young woman who
had greeted them.

Megan. Megan James.

"Tim, I need you to find whatever personal information you can dig up on Megan James. She's a student
assistant to Dr. Jacob Tanner at the college. In fact, I
need both her and his addresses as quickly as possible.
I don't care what avenue you need to use to get the information for me, just get it as quickly as possible."

As Tim began to type, Alexander jumped to his feet
and quickly pulled his phone from his pocket. It took
him only minutes to call Matt and Frank and tell them
to get back to the war room immediately.

Although every nerve in his body screamed for action, he knew he needed backup if what he believed was
true. He'd gone off half-cocked in the Gilmer case and
the result had been tragic.

Of course, in that particular case it wouldn't have
mattered if he'd had a dozen or a thousand agents with
him. The simple truth was that they had been too late
to save Kelly. He would not, he *could* not, be too late
to save Georgina.

Throughout the long night, he and Nicholas had
made peace. Nicholas had been appalled by the fact
that Alexander had entertained any doubt about his
commitment to his job, about his loyalty to the team.

He'd told Alexander how his family had spent the first five years of his life living in a shanty in the swamp, and then his father had gotten a job that had allowed them to move into the city. Nicholas had worked hard to overcome his early beginnings.

The young agent was ambitious and bright. All he needed was some seasoning, and Alexander thought he'd already learned some valuable lessons and would eventually be quite successful within the agency.

Right now, Nicholas and lessons were the very last things on Alexander's mind as he paced the floor waiting for Matt and Frank to arrive.

He needed them to get here as quickly as possible. He had no idea what part Megan had played in the crimes, but it was an indisputable fact that she had been the lure that had drawn him out of the house and onto his porch so that Tanner could dart him into unconsciousness.

Tim got the addresses for both Megan James and Jacob Tanner and handed them to Alex at the same time Matt walked in. "What's up?" he asked.

"I think we've got him." As he explained to Matt what he'd remembered, Frank arrived and within minutes the three of them were on their way to Tanner's off-campus town house.

"If he's leading the double life I believe he is, then he should be at home at this hour of the morning." Every nerve in Alexander's body burned, every muscle tensed.

He could be wrong. They'd all been wrong when they'd rushed to the old structure at the back of Baker's Bayou. He'd never considered that Bob might have a partner, but there was no question in his mind now that it had been Megan who had lured him outside.

He now had a perfect memory of looking out of his peephole in the door and seeing Megan James standing there. He'd felt no fear, only curiosity as to what had brought her to his home.

When he remembered meeting the young woman, he had seen the hero worship she had for her boss. It only made sense that if she were a part of this, then Tanner was Bob.

However, there was no way to be absolutely certain. It was possible that Megan was a puppet for some other sick twist…maybe another student who wanted to become infamous.

As Matt drove toward Jacob Tanner's town house, Alexander found himself second-guessing the move. Maybe they should have confronted Megan first. He voiced his concerns aloud, but both of the other men thought his first reaction, to get to Tanner first, was the right one.

"If nothing else we bring him in and get him behind bars. We'll have twelve hours to sort it out before we have to bring some sort of charges against him or release him," Matt said.

"I hope to hell we solve this long before another twelve hours," Alexander replied. He couldn't imagine going another hour without having Georgina back safe and sound, and he knew wherever she was, the other missing people would be there as well.

Jacob Tanner lived in an affluent area within walking distance of the college. The town houses were redbrick with white trim, the lawns neatly manicured and the overall maintenance of the dozen or so town houses fresh.

Teachers and professors mostly lived here, with easy

access to the campus and the respectable address to give them additional status.

Matt parked in front of the curb of the professor's place and the three men quickly exited the car. Alexander pulled his gun as he approached the front door. "Matt, go around to the back door. I don't want him making some kind of escape."

Matt nodded and left the two. When he had disappeared, Alexander nodded to Nicholas, who drew his weapon and held it at the ready. None of them knew if Tanner was dangerous or not.

Alexander intended to take no chances. If Tanner was Bob, then Alexander would not give him an opportunity to take him down again. There would be no darts in the back with this encounter. There would only be a gun to the chest and it would be Alexander's gun doing the pointing.

His watch read exactly seven o'clock when he knocked on the front door. It was early enough that Tanner shouldn't have left for classes yet. "Maybe he's a sound sleeper," Nicholas said after they'd waited several moments.

Alexander knocked again, this time loud enough to awaken the neighbors. He leaned with his ear against the door but could hear nothing that might indicate anyone was inside. He knocked a final time and then turned to Nicholas.

"I don't think he's here. Walk around and check the windows and then get Matt and we'll head over to Megan's place. Maybe she knows where the good professor would be at this time of the morning."

Nicholas nodded and Alexander watched as he, too

disappeared around the side of the town house. There was a front window and he moved to peer inside. He holstered his gun and cupped his hands to allow him to see a neat and tidy living room.

He saw no shadows lurking in the room, nothing to indicate that anyone was inside. The garages for the town houses were completely enclosed and without windows, making it impossible for them to check to see if a car was parked inside.

Matt and Nicholas joined him on the sidewalk. "I didn't see anyone through the back door," Matt said.

"And same with me in the windows I looked in. I'd say he's not here." Nicholas frowned thoughtfully. "I wonder just how close he might be with his assistant? Close enough to spend his nights in her bed?"

"Let's go find out," Alexander said.

Alexander read out Megan's address as Matt pulled away from the curb. "She'll be arrested no matter what," he said. "If nothing else she's an accomplice to Georgina's kidnapping and the attack on me."

"Then it's possible she won't be home, either," Matt said. "Why would she stick around if she knows you can identify her as an accomplice?"

"I don't know. I can't figure out why she would have let herself be seen by me at all," Alexander admitted. It was a puzzle he had yet to put together.

"Maybe she's a victim, too. Maybe Tanner forced her to participate in luring you out and then he kidnapped her as well," Matt suggested.

"That really doesn't fit the profile," Nicholas replied. "But then again, I guess it would be a mistake to discount anything."

"Maybe she's going to try to convince me it wasn't her at the door, but there's no doubt in my mind that it was her." Alexander pulled his cell phone from his pocket and dialed Tim's cell.

"Tim, talk to Judge Warner and get us search warrants for the addresses you gave me earlier. He's a sympathetic judge, but make sure you tell him we believe the two people who reside at the addresses are a killer holding hostages and his accomplice. See if you can get it done in the next thirty minutes and have somebody from the team meet us at Megan's address with the paperwork."

"No fruit of the poisonous tree in this case," Matt observed.

"We play everything by the book," Alexander said. "I don't want us to make a single mistake that might poison the case we have to build to make sure our Bob and anyone else helping him spends the rest of their lives in jail."

As he dropped the phone back into his pocket, his nerves jangled inside him and his heart beat out the cadence of Georgina's name.

Megan James's apartment building was a far cry from Tanner's town house. Although the outside appeared fairly nice, the hallway smelled of sweaty gym clothes, stale smoke and the day after parties.

Once again Alexander pulled his gun and then knocked on the door. Matt and Nicholas stood just behind him. Alexander's stomach clenched as the door opened to reveal a young woman with long red hair and clad in a robe. Her blue eyes nearly popped out of her head as she saw the men with their guns.

"Wha…what's going on?" she asked.

"We're FBI agents. We understood this was Megan James's apartment," Alexander said.

"It is. I'm her roommate." Her eyes were still huge even as Alexander holstered his gun.

"Where is Megan?" he asked.

"She left just a little while ago to head over to the Humanities building. Professor Tanner called her late last night and told her his mother was ill and she should take over teaching his classes for the next week or so."

"Thanks," Alexander replied and turned to leave.

"Is Megan in some kind of trouble?" the woman asked.

"Let's just say I'd be looking for a new roommate if I were you," Matt said as the three of them hurried back to their car.

"This is so bizarre," Nicholas said a few minutes later as they strode toward the Humanities building. "How can she believe she isn't in any trouble? How can she possibly explain being at your house last night?"

"I'd like to know how Tanner is going to explain having a sick mother when his mother died years ago," Alexander said tersely. He was ready for this to end. He made a quick call to Tim to let him know they were headed to the college campus.

When they reached Tanner's office door, Alexander didn't bother to knock. He opened the door to see Megan at the desk. Her eyes widened as the three men came through the doorway.

"Agent Harkins," she said in surprise. "I'm afraid if you're looking for Professor Tanner again, you're going to have a long wait. His mother is ill and he's left town."

Alexander stared at her, wondering if she was completely psychotic. She didn't appear to be concerned that he was here and acted like she hadn't seen him since the last time he and Georgina had been here to speak to Tanner.

"That's funny since his mother died a long time ago. What I'd like to know is what you were doing on my doorstep last night." Had it only been last night that he'd held Georgina in his arms and told her how much he loved her?

Megan frowned. "Me? At your house last night? I don't know what you're talking about." She gave him a confident smile that suddenly boiled his blood. "Surely you're mistaken, Agent Harkins, I don't even know where you live. Did anyone besides you see me there?"

The tension that had coiled inside him snapped. He motioned toward Matt. "Take her into custody."

As Matt moved forward and pulled handcuffs from his pocket, alligator tears began to track down Megan's cheeks. "Please, I don't know what's going on. Why would you think I was at your house? What is it you think I've done wrong?"

Matt cuffed her hands behind her back as she continued to cry. "This is all a mistake. Please, explain to me what's happening. I don't understand."

Alexander motioned for Matt to get her out of the office. Nicholas gazed at Alexander with a wry, tight smile. "So now we know her defense. There were three people at your house last night. One of them isn't talking and her story is she was never there. The word of a drugged-up FBI agent against a sobbing, innocent teacher's aide." He shrugged. "It might work for her. I've seen defense attorneys work with less."

Alexander's phone rang. Terry was downstairs with their search warrants in hand. Alexander and Nicholas took the stairs two at a time down and out of the building where Matt had loaded a still weeping Megan into the back of Terry's car.

"Tanner's place," Alexander said as the three agents once again were in the car. "My gut says we won't find anything of use in Megan's place, but if Tanner is Bob, then he might have something in his house that will confirm not only that fact but might also point to where he is holding the hostages."

Aware of the minutes…hours lost, Alexander wished he could freeze time. It was already nearly ten. Too many hours had passed. They had to find something at Tanner's. He had to pray that the answers were there.

When they reached Tanner's town house, Alexander knocked on the door once and then he and Matt threw their shoulders against it to pop the lock. It took three tries before the door sprang open and they all entered.

With guns drawn, they cleared each room one at a time, then certain that Tanner was no place in the house, they began their search for some sort of evidence.

"Matt, you take the kitchen and dining area. Nicholas, check out the master bedroom. I'm going to go over everything in his office," Alexander said. "Try to do as little damage as possible but don't leave a single place unsearched."

The second bedroom had been turned into a home office and the first thing he did was sit at the desk and begin going methodically through the drawers. He didn't know what exactly he was looking for, but knew he'd recognize it on sight.

The first desk drawer held pens and paper clips and the office materials that were usually in a desk. The side drawer held hanging file folders that contained what appeared to be old lesson plans.

Aware of time ticking by, he quickly searched each and every file. He found nothing in the desk of interest. He opened up the laptop on the desktop and found it password protected. He shut it down, intending to take it to Tim when they left here.

With his heart ticking off the time…precious time that was moving far too fast, he checked the bookcase that held only books from top to bottom.

Hearing nothing from the other agents, he sat back down at the desk and leaned back, a well of grief threatening to pull him in and drown him.

His good friend, Jackson, six other innocent people and Georgina, all gone…vanished as if lifted from the face of the earth. And the only clue they had was that they were certain Bob had sprung from the swamp.

He frowned as he realized he'd been staring at a framed 8 x 10 photo on the wall opposite him. It was a picture of a swamp and what appeared to be an old, crumbling concrete building peeking through the trees.

He jumped up from his chair and grabbed the photo from the wall. "Matt, Nicholas," he called. When the two agents entered the office, he held out the photo. "Either one of you know where this might be?"

"I have no idea," Matt replied.

"Doesn't look familiar to me," Nicholas added.

Alexander set the photo on the edge of the desk and

ripped off the frame and glass. This was it. He knew that this was where Tanner was keeping the captives.

The pit of his stomach burned as he thought of Tanner sitting at his desk and perhaps sipping a fine wine while staring at the place where he'd stashed his victims. He could just imagine the pleasure that swept through the madman when he viewed this photo.

Once the picture was out of the frame, Alexander looked at the back, releasing a small gasp of relief as he saw writing on the bottom.

"Baton Rouge Institute for the Criminally Insane," he read aloud. "Shelter Swamp, Baton Rouge." He looked at the two men. "This is it. Matt, get on the phone to Tim and get us a location for Shelter Swamp."

"Nicholas, call in the troops, have them meet us here." Alexander's hands trembled too much to make the calls. He clutched the photo tightly, knowing in his very gut that this was the place and Tanner was their man.

But it would take them an hour or so to pull everything together and get there, and he had no idea how long Tanner had been gone or if he was with the victims.

They were closing in, but would they be in time?

Chapter Fourteen

One thing Georgina realized while she sat on her bunk and listened to the conversations of the others was that they had formed a bond, a bond that would see them through the rest of their lives…if they got the opportunity to live the rest of their lives.

The second thing she'd realized was that she believed she would die here. She knew the lack of clues the team had, the vast area of swampland they had to explore. The odds of the captives being found were minimal in her mind.

In facing death, she realized how much she wanted to live…to really live, not just go through the motions as she'd been doing for most of her life.

Alex's words of love had done so much to soothe the wounds that her childhood had left behind. She realized she'd been playing a loop in her head for years, telling herself she was a failure, that she was no good to anyone. Words from her past that had made her believe she was not good enough for Alex, that he would be much better off without her.

She had told him that maybe he needed therapy to get over his guilt concerning the Gilmer case, but she was the one who needed therapy to finally heal the inner child inside her who had been abused and abandoned.

Now it was too late for therapy, it was too late to tell Alex just how much she loved him and that she did want a do-over with him. With the self-realizations that had come from this case, she felt better, stronger and was ready to accept Alex's love and build a life with him.

She supposed she should thank Bob for making her immerse herself in her past. She had come out stronger on the other side. Unfortunately, the only way she might thank Bob was if he released everyone and then sacrificed himself by falling into the swamp and drowning.

As if summoned by her very thoughts, the door on the opposite side of the room opened and Bob walked in. As usual his face was covered by a ski mask. He grabbed the folding chair and then carried it over in front of her cell, opened it and sat.

"Hello, Georgina." His voice seemed to hold genuine affection.

"Hello, Bob." Her voice did not.

"I thought we'd have a little chat. I've so enjoyed speaking to you in the past," he said.

"First I'd like you to just answer one question for me. Why? Why are you doing this? Why do you want to be a serial killer?" She needed to know the reason for all of this before she died.

"I not only want to be the best serial killer in the world, but I also want to be the best teacher." He reached up and pulled off his ski mask and she was stunned to see Professor Jacob Tanner's boyish face.

His unmasking of himself also rang a death knell for

them all. There was no way he'd allow any of them to live now that he'd shown them his face.

"I lied to you when I told you I killed my parents," he said. "I've never killed anyone before, but I've dreamed about it, I've obsessed about it since I was a very young boy."

"Then let us all go. Nobody is dead yet and we'll all ask the judge to go easy on you." She got up from her cot and stood in front of him, her hands gripping the iron bars. "You're an esteemed professor, Jacob. You don't have to do this. You don't have to become a killer."

"Oh, but I do." His blue eyes shone with a brilliance that could only be madness. He leaned forward, the intensity of his gaze sickening her. "How can I teach my students about serial killers without creating death myself? How can I tell them about the power you feel when you watch the life drain from a victim's eyes, when you place your hand on their chest and feel their very last breath?"

"You're crazy," Jackson said.

"Shut up," Tanner replied as he pulled a gun from his pocket and pointed it at Jackson. "I'm ready to begin my new life, as a brilliant teacher and as a killer. I was going to give Georgina the honor of being my first victim, but I'm not adverse to changing my mind and picking you."

"Then pick me," Jackson said as he grabbed the bars of his cage and shook them like an enraged gorilla.

"Stop it," Georgina said frantically. "Jackson, don't try to be a hero. Professor Tanner and I have a relationship that none of you have, that none of you could possibly understand."

"That's right." Tanner lowered the gun and smiled at her.

"Did you lie about your childhood, too?" she asked. At least as long as he was talking, he wasn't killing anyone.

His eyes darkened. "No, I didn't lie about that. I grew up in the swamp and my father was a brutal man who drank too much and then beat me and my mother half senseless. I knew early on that the only way I was going to get out of the swamp and escape him—escape them—was through education. I worked hard and got scholarships that saw me through all of my schooling."

"Where are your parents now?" she asked.

"Probably living in the same old shack where I grew up. When I left for college, I never looked back. I never went back there. For all I know, they both could be dead." He straightened tall in the chair with obvious pride. "I was better than that. I was better than both of them."

"You've done so well, Jacob. Why screw it all up now?" she asked.

Once again his eyes glittered with ill-concealed excitement. "I'm not screwing anything up now. I'm just becoming what I was always meant to be. I've learned everything I need to know from these men and women. How can I screw up when I have all I need to know how to kill unmercifully and never be caught?"

"Eventually you will get caught," Georgina replied. "We always catch them. You'll get arrogant and that will lead to you getting sloppy and you'll make a mistake."

"You're wrong. I've been trained by the very best." He gestured down the row of cells. "It was easy for me to pick them out. Michelle sent me her book chapter by chapter long before it was ever published. I used her research for her book to find three sterling examples of profilers to help teach me."

"You must have been quite amused when Agent Harkins and I came to talk to you about Michelle and Roger," she replied.

He laughed, a sound that was jarringly pleasant given the dire circumstances and the surroundings. "I have to admit I was quite amused, although I admired the fact that you'd homed in on Michelle and Roger so quickly."

"Why me? How did you find me? My phone number and address?" The questions had haunted her.

"I saw you that night at Michelle's book signing. I heard you and Agent Harkins introduce yourselves to Michelle. The internet is a wonderful tool if you can pay for certain services. It only took me minutes to have your phone number and address at my disposal."

"Let Macy go," she said softly. "She can't hurt you, Jacob. She's just a little girl. She deserves to have a long and happy life."

"Not all people get happy childhoods—you know that as well as I do," Tanner replied. "From what you told me, you suffered tremendously as a child."

"That's right," she said, owning the truth for what felt like the very first time in her life. "I was physically, mentally and emotionally terrorized from the time I was born until I was sixteen, both by my parents and by my older sisters. But that didn't make me want to kill people. I chose to turn my life around, to make something of myself. And you've done that, Professor. Your students adore you. Your classes are the most popular on campus. Why can't that be enough?"

"Because it's not," he cried in sudden rage. "I have a plan that will cause people to tremble when they think of me, to have nightmares about me. I want to make headlines and I want to kill. I have a bloodlust, Georgina, and finally I'm going to satisfy it. I'm done killing gators in the swamp. I want to kill people."

He stood abruptly and kicked his chair back. He waved his gun in the air and Georgina backed away from the bars. Danger crackled in the air and the only sound was a faint whimper from Macy.

Tanner laughed again, knowing that he was the one in control, knowing that he struck fear in each and every person in the room. His laughter held a sickening glee that Georgina feared would linger in her head even as she died.

"I'm tired of talking," Tanner said. He stalked up the line of cells, pointing his gun into each one, obviously reveling in the fear he struck in each of his captives' hearts.

He finally stopped and stood once again in front of Georgina's cell. "It's time to quit talking and start acting." He raised his gun and pointed it at her.

"Freeze!" The achingly familiar voice came from the doorway at the same time Tanner's gun discharged and a bullet slammed into her chest, throwing her backward to the floor as pain seared through her.

She was vaguely aware of the sound of other shots and then Alex was at her cell door, yelling for somebody to get the key, to get medical help. Frantic, he was so frantic and she wanted to tell him to calm down, that everything was going to be all right.

She knew that something important was happening, but she couldn't remember what. Cold. Why was she so cold? She wanted to tell Alex to hurry, to come and warm her in his big strong arms, but the words refused to form on her lips no matter how hard she tried to speak.

Finally he was there next to her and she was shocked to see tears trekking down his cheeks. "Hang on, baby," he said. "Help is on the way."

She managed to raise her hand and place it on the side of his beautiful, handsome face. "Do-over," she managed to say, her voice coming from very far away as darkness sprang out of nowhere and took possession of her.

IS THIS WHAT DEATH WAS LIKE? Georgina's thoughts raced as she remained unmoving, with her eyes closed, in a soft, comfortable bed. But, surely, death didn't involve the soft steady sound of deep snoring.

Familiar snoring. She opened her eyes and realized she wasn't dead, but rather was in a hospital room. The snoring came from an obviously exhausted Alex, who was slumped in a chair nearby and sleeping deeply.

She closed her eyes once again and thought about what had happened before she'd fallen unconscious. She'd been shot, but Alex had saved her. He'd saved them all.

She remembered the shots that had rung through the structure as she'd fallen to the floor of her cell. There was no doubt in her mind that Professor Jacob Tanner, FBI-trained serial killer, was dead, but little Macy would hopefully live a happy and wonderful life with her parents who so loved her.

Georgina was in pain, but it was manageable. She wondered what medical magic had been done to her in order to keep her here on earth.

She opened her eyes again and turned to look at Alex, his eyes drifted open, going from a sleepy blue to the blue of an electric charge.

"Georgina!" He jumped from the chair and was by her side in two short strides. "Thank God." He grabbed on to her hand and squeezed tight, his eyes moist with unshed tears.

He looked awful. His eyes were red-rimmed and his jaw sported a growth of dark whiskers. Stress lines dug into his skin, making him look half-sick.

She licked her chapped lips and realized her throat was sore. He seemed to know exactly what she needed as he grabbed a glass of water from a nearby tray and gently lifted her head so she could take a little sip of the cool liquid from a thin straw.

"I've got to let the doctor know that you're awake," he said.

"Wait," the word croaked out of her. "How long have I been here?"

"Two long, terrible days."

"You look like crap."

He laughed and some of the tension eased from his face, from his shoulders. "Honey, you should look in a mirror right about now."

A nurse walked in and stopped in surprise. "You're awake. I'll go let the doctor know." As she turned on squeaky heels and left the room, Georgina looked back at Alex.

"What's the damage?" she asked.

"Two broken ribs, one destroyed spleen…"

"And a partridge in a pear tree," she quipped.

He smiled and once again squeezed her hand. "Now I know for sure you're going to be fine." The smile fell as he released a ragged sigh. "I thought I'd lost you, Georgina. I thought I'd lost you forever."

"You can't get rid of me so easily."

"I don't want to get rid of you ever," he replied. "Do you remember what you said to me after you'd been shot?" His beautiful blue eyes gazed at her intently.

She frowned, trying to remember those moments before she'd fallen unconscious. And then she remembered and she grasped the moment in both hands, knowing what she wanted more than anything else in the world.

"Do-over. I told you I wanted a do-over."

He nodded, the tension creeping back across his handsome features as his eyes darkened. "I didn't know exactly what you meant, whether you wanted a do-over of the night you were kidnapped, or if you wanted a do-over with me…with us."

She could tell he was holding his breath, hoping that she answered the way he wanted her to. "I probably need some therapy," she said tentatively.

He nodded. "We can do that. We can do anything together, Georgina. We belong together."

She gazed at him, falling into the love that shone from his eyes, believing in the love that was in her heart for him. She wanted to be the one he turned to in the night when demons chased him in his dreams. And she wanted him to be the one to hold her when her own darkness tried to claim her.

"I'm good enough," she said.

"Damn straight you are. You deserve to be happy, Georgina, and I promise you that I will spend every day for the rest of my life working to keep you happy."

"Alex, I was a fool to walk out on you…on us. I didn't believe I deserved to be happy, but after hearing what Tanner said about his past and seeing what hanging on to that pain created in him, I know I'm better than that. I need to let go of my past to have my future and I want that future to be with you."

He leaned forward and gave her a gentle kiss. "I want to grab you and hug you tight right now, but I don't think that would be a very good idea."

"That is definitely a bad idea," a man who was obviously a doctor said as he walked into the room.

He nodded at Alex and then walked to the side of Georgina's bed. "Georgina, I'm Dr. Mac Evans." He placed a gentle hand on her wrist and checked her pulse, then stood back and smiled. "You gave us all quite a scare for a little while, but it looks like you're going to be just fine."

"Great, when can I get out of here?" she asked.

"We need to keep you for a couple of days, and then, depending on how fast you're healing, we should be able to cut you loose," Dr. Evans replied.

"I'm a very quick healer," she replied and her gaze went to Alex. "Especially when I have something to heal for."

His eyes burned with the fiery light of desire, with the sweet promise of love, and Georgina knew in her heart that their do-over would last forever.

"Aye, lass."

The preacher cleared his throat when Iain started to lean in to kiss Emily. He gave his little speech about who was marrying and then asked who gave the bride to the man. Robbie began to step forward but jerked to a halt when a deep voice sounded from behind them.

"I believe that should be my job, young sir."

"Grandfather?"

Emily turned around and stared at the big man standing in the doorway to the parlor. She shook free of her shock and ran to him. When she reached him he opened his arms and she ran right into them. Clutching him tightly she tried to control her tears.

"How did you get here?" she asked.

"Constance told me. Then I received your letter about Annabel and David." He sighed. "They are really dead? Killed by Albert?"

"Yes, Grandfather."

"I should have heeded you when you said he murdered your parents but it was so hard to think the boy I raised could do such a thing. So, after the letter came with the sad news about Annabel and her man, I spoke with Constance and she gave me her information that had come right from Annabel and I set right out immediately." He looked over her head to frown at Iain. "Seems I came at an opportune time."

Tugging her grandfather over to Iain, Emily introduced the pair. "I am so happy you are here for my wedding, Grandfather."

Iain looked at the man, and decided he did not look as he expected a duke to look. He was tall and broad-shouldered. There did not appear to be any fat on the man, just muscle. He was also very handsome for a man in his sixties, with steel-gray eyes and hair that was still more golden than white. The hand that shook his was strong and calloused.

"Your Grace," he said politely.

"Who are all those lads behind you?"

"My brothers Matthew, Geordie, Nigel, Lachlan, and Duncan. The two fellows with the black hair are Owen and David Powell. And the fellow who was about to give me my bride is my brother Robbie. I gather ye will take the job now."

"Well," began the man, and he glanced at Emily, who quickly slid her arm through his.

"Yes, he will," Emily said. "This is the man who saved me and Neddy, Grandfather. This is the place where I have been staying and they fought off Albert's men. Twice. We have so much to tell you but I would like to get married first, please."

"You are sure of this, sweetheart?" the duke asked quietly, searching her face for any hint of doubt.

"Very sure, Grandfather."

To his relief, Iain soon found himself kissing the bride, the vows said and rings exchanged. Confident that there would be no trouble about it now, he moved everyone into the dining room. Neddy walked next to Emily but his gaze stayed on the duke.

"Neddy, that man is your mama's grandfather," Emily said gently. "Perhaps you could be a gentleman and lead him into the dining room."

"It is right there." The boy pointed at the door they were about to enter and Iain heard the duke choke back a laugh.

"Then escort him to his seat, love."

The dining room was packed and Iain was astonished at the amount of food Mrs. O'Neal and Emily had made. The woman even found out that the duke had six riders with him and got Mabel to help her take food out to them. As Iain attempted to eat the duke kept him answering questions about what he did, his life, and his history. As he was beginning to get somewhat irritated at the constant barrage of questions, Emily turned her grandfather's attention to Neddy.

"I am so sorry," Emily whispered to Iain.

"Nay, lass." He brushed a kiss over her mouth and grimaced at the cheers from the people all around them. "He is doing what most family would do. I just am nay in the mood for it. I have a lot better things to do and think about," he added in a whisper.

Emily tried hard not to blush but knew she was not fully successful when Maggie winked at her. She was so happy to see her grandfather although she worried that such a journey would have been hard on a man his age. Surreptitiously she looked him over carefully. He did not look weary or ill so she told herself to stop worrying.

A lot of time passed with so many people to speak to and the abundance of laughter but finally Iain stood up and started to lead her out of the room. Everyone leapt to their feet and the women got in front of them to pelt them with seeds. Emily laughed because they were only going to the room the brothers had added, one that was large and private on the far side of the house. Emily took the time to speak to Mrs. O'Neal and make sure her grandfather and his men were seen to before Iain dragged her away. She wanted to go with him but she also wanted to visit with her grandfather.

"Ye can visit with him tomorrow," Iain said as he led her into their room. "Tonight is mine. Look at what I have made for us."

Emily shed her veil and looked around. It was a

very good-sized room with a sitting room attached
and a small room for a bath and the close-stool. One
could still smell the freshness of the wood. On the
floor were beautifully woven carpets and over the fireplace in the bedroom was a picture of the spot on the
trail she had so loved. Then he led her to yet another
room and let her look around.

"This is for when we have a bairn."

"This was a lot to add in just a few weeks, Iain. I
had not expected it to be all finished."

"Still a wee bit of finishing needed but we got the
wood and such a while back so that saved time."

"What do you mean 'a while back'?"

He reached up to take the hair clips from her hair.
"I told myself it was time to add something to the
house, a place where I could get away from the crowd
and all that. But not long after I met ye I think I kenned
exactly what I was making. A place where ye and I can
get away together."

"A little house within a house."

"Aye, now let us go and christen our new bed."

"Matthew's work?" she asked as she stared at the
big bed made of a dark wood.

"Aye." He started to undo her gown. "He has some
finishing work to do on it as well."

"It is beautiful." She noticed he had taken his
jacket off and reached out to undo the buttons on
his shirt. "Do we have to go back outside to get into
the main house?"

"Nay. There is a door into the kitchen in the sitting
room."

He gently pushed her back toward the bed until
the edge hit the back of her knees and she sat down.
Iain tugged off her gown then knelt to remove her
shoes and stockings. By the time he had her stripped

to her shift, he noticed his hands were shaking. This time, he thought, was so much more important to him.

Knowing how she still suffered from modesty he left her shift on her as he pushed her down on to the bed. He began to shed his clothes, loving the way she watched him, her eyes growing warmer with each piece of clothing he tossed aside. Iain had never given much thought to his body, but she made him think he might be handsome. He was in her eyes and that was all he cared about.

Once on the bed with her he kissed her and slowly undid her shift. Emily was stroking his chest and back as he stripped the shift off her leaving her beautifully naked before him. He kissed her throat, savoring the taste of her soft skin, and then began to move slowly down to her breasts. The soft cries she gave as he kissed her there and then took a nipple deep into his mouth had him grow even more in need of her. She arched into his kiss and thrust her fingers in his hair.

Emily murmured her regret as he kissed his way down her body because he moved out of her reach. She liked stroking the warm skin of his back, even daringly moving her hands over his taut backside. She shivered as he stroked and kissed her legs. When he moved his kisses back up and began to love her with his mouth, she clutched his head but was not sure if she was trying to push him away or hold him close.

Then she began to feel that tightening she now recognized and tried to tug him back into her arms. He neatly avoided her attempts until she was so caught up in the desire flooding her body she did not even care to try. Then the tautness inside her snapped and pleasure flooded her. She cried out his name as he surged

up and over her and drove himself inside her. That
made the pleasure linger and wash over her a second
time but this time he went with her.

As the fierce wave of passion ebbed, she clung to
him and tried to catch her breath. She could feel the
heat of his own ragged breathing against her neck.
Then a strange banging noise startled her and she
tightened her grip on him.

"What is that?"

"Our guests having some fun tormenting the new
bride and groom. I am nay sure what it is supposed to
accomplish except make sure ye stay awake to keep at
it." He smiled against her breast when she giggled.

"Are you supposed to do anything?"

He shrugged even as he stood up to tug on his pants
and throw on his shirt. "Your grandfather is going to
think all Americans are mad," he said as he walked
to the window and opened it to stick his head out.
"Are ye finished?"

That brought more risqué comments than he
wanted but they moved away. Iain yelled after them
that they better not drink all his liquor, shut the
window, and then walked back to the bed. Emily was
sitting up and clutching the sheet to her chest.

"Saying that will probably just encourage them to
try to do it," she said.

He stripped off his clothes, crawled back into bed,
and then tugged her into his arms. "I ken it but it will
mean they are too drunk to come and bother us."

"How very sneaky of you."

"Aye." He kissed her. "Ye are beautiful, love. Beautiful and so warm in a man's arms. Only mine though."

"Only yours." She kissed his cheek.

"Right answer." He tickled her and while she tried
to recover from that he got up and fetched a wet cloth.

She could not help but blush as he cleaned her off, then himself before putting the washrag away. It was just so personal yet he insisted on doing it every time. She had the feeling she would regret it if he did not do it so did not complain, just welcomed him back into her arms when he got back into bed.

"What about Neddy?" she asked.

"Mrs. O'Neal is keeping watch on him tonight."

"I was rather thinking of the rest of the nights."

"Nay sure, love. He is a good lad but I have a need to be shagging my wife whenever I want to." He laughed and caught her arm as she swung at him. "We will figure something out. There is the bairn's room if he has to be near you."

She nodded. "He is just used to being in a room with me and I do not want him to get even more upset about this marriage."

Iain chuckled as he recalled his confrontations with the boy after he had announced that he and Emily were getting married. "He will settle, love. I told him I wasnae taking ye away from him, just sharing ye. Making us three instead of just two. That seemed to calm him down."

"I hope so."

"Dinnae fret over him. He speaks his mind to ye so ye willnae have to play at guessing what ails him. I also think once he understood what was happening, he began to calm down a bit."

She nodded and began to stroke his chest. "I was not going to give up marrying you just because a three-year-old child was mad. I love you."

He kissed her, pleased that she said it so freely. He wanted to make love to her again but thought she might need a little rest before he was all over her again. Then her soft small hand slid over his belly and she wrapped those slender fingers around him. Iain decided she had rested enough.

Emily woke to a desire that was fire in her blood. Iain was settled between her legs and his tongue was driving her into a frenzy of need. She opened to him and just luxuriated in the feeling he stirred within her. When he kissed his way up her body she was more than ready for him, but he took his time. Then he thrust into her and she grabbed him to hold him in place, a small part of her fevered mind noting that she was scratching him but she really could not be bothered to find out for sure. Then their passion crested together and she hung on as they both tumbled.

It was several moments before she noticed he was rather heavy. She looked at him sprawled on top of her and she smiled a little. It was heady to think she had put him in such a state. He finally rolled to the side and she moved to sprawl up against him.

"Loving ye is going to be the death of me."

"Well, we cannot be doing this every night or we will both be too tired to do anything else."

"Fine with me." He smiled when she giggled. "Ah, lass, I cannae believe ye said aye to me. I was a miserable beau."

"I thought you were just fine."

"That is good because I doubt I will suddenly get the skill to do much wooing over the years. I never realized how hard it is. I think ye will have to be the one to teach our children."

"Children?"

"Was that something I should have got sorted out before we wed? Dinnae ye want any?"

"Of course. I just had not given it much thought. Only time I thought of it was when we had not even spoken of marriage and I briefly feared bearing a child with no husband."

"I would have wed you."

"And I would have always wondered if it was only because of the child."

He grimaced. "Aye, I can see that. But ye ken now that I love ye and this marriage will stand. Aye?"

She brushed a kiss over his mouth. "Aye." She grinned briefly. "And I would like to have children with you. Just not sure I am eager to have seven boys."

He laughed. "I dinnae think that will be a problem. And ye will have some girls. I am fair sure of it."

"A girl with six big uncles, a cousin, and assorted other men and boys keeping a watch over her. Not sure I would want to do that to any girl."

Iain laughed. "It would be a hard road for the wee lass." He kissed her cheek. "But I do think I want a wee lass with your fair hair and bonnie eyes."

"How about we just enjoy being the two of us for a while?"

"A very good idea, Mrs. MacEnroy."

Chapter Twenty-One

Two years later

"He said he would be here. We had such a nice visit when he came for the wedding and he asked if I planned to have children because he wanted to be sure to be there for my firstborn," Emily said, looking out through the open gates from where she stood in the doorway. "He wanted to see the birth of our son and I wrote him as soon as I knew I was carrying your child. I cannot think of what has happened to him. He always does what he says he will."

Iain walked up behind her, put his arms around her, and placed his hands on her belly. "It will be a wee lass."

He grinned when she sighed. They had been having the same disagreement for nine long months, starting it before he had even realized she was carrying his child. Mrs. O'Neal was kept busy judging every change in Emily and still had not decided what she was having. Emily felt it was sure to be a boy because he had six brothers. He simply felt it was time for a change and, he admitted, he enjoyed poking at her conviction that it was a boy.

"And then there are the troubles he may have to go through." She twisted her hands as she fretted. "I had not realized how wide it had spread or how vicious it had become when I wrote him." She turned in his arms and looked up at him, her well-rounded belly pushing her from him. "There is so much that could happen to him as he travels here."

"I dinnae think traveling across England is all that safe, either, love."

"No, but they are not a country torn apart all trying to kill each other. Not for a few hundred years anyway."

"A lot of people travel about the country still and do so safely. I agree, it is a bad time but that doesnae mean he will suffer for it."

She rubbed her belly and thought on warning him that she was fairly certain she was in labor. Inwardly she then shook her head. The minute she said anything he would get all commanding, ordering everyone about and making her go lie down. She could have hours yet before she gave birth and she did not want to spend them all confined to her bed.

The ache had been there when she had woken up in the morning. Emily had asked every woman she knew who had borne a child what their birthing pains had been like and how they had begun, how they felt as they strengthened and how they knew it was getting near time to have the baby. They had all been honest with her even though they had been reluctant at first, afraid of terrifying her. She had convinced them that she was fully aware that birthing a child was a painful business and all she wanted to know was how painful and how to recognize when she was actually in labor.

Right now all she was truly worried about was where her grandfather was. There had not been the time to warn him about the troubles. She had written to him as soon as she had realized the scope of the rift that had split the country but mail was neither swift nor sure. Emily doubted her letter would have gotten to him in time to stop him.

Iain's hand covered hers and she realized she had been rubbing her stomach the whole time she had been thinking. She glanced up at him and he was frowning down at her belly. Curious as to what he might be seeing she looked down. The man's hand was still resting there and she knew her belly was harder than it had been, the baby still. Emily was not sure he could feel that ache that had woken her up this morning but she began to wonder.

"Emily?" he said quietly.

She returned her gaze to the gates and wondered what she could say only to tense as a big, fancy carriage came rolling through. A carriage she knew very well. Her grandfather had had his own people build it for him and it had a lot of comforts from the fold-down table to the seats that were easily changed to beds. The people who got to see the inside all wanted to buy it or have him make one for them.

"He is here," she cried out softly, pleased to see that her grandfather had arrived and eager to see he was hale.

His Grace climbed out of the carriage the moment it stopped and she sighed with relief. The man was accustomed to his title working to keep him relatively protected but that title was not worth much here. His mode of travel, however, could all too easily make him a tempting target for thieves in this country of which they had far too many and all armed.

"Good Lord, girl," her grandfather said laughingly as he stepped up to give her a hug and kiss her on the cheek, "are you sure you carry but the one?"

"Yes. Only one. I tried to get a letter to you to tell you not to come. The troubles . . ."

"I know about them. It is going to be a long bloody fight. Always is when a country is fighting itself." He shook Iain's hand. "Trying to keep out of the way here?"

"As much as possible, aye."

"Smart man."

"Come in and we will get you something to eat and drink, Grandfather."

"That would be very welcome." He put his arm around her shoulders as they walked inside. "Where is my heir?"

"Being fetched from the yard. If you knew about it all, why did you travel here? You should have waited until it passed."

"Emily, wars are unpredictable. Occasionally you get a short one that doesn't leave everyone bruised and bloody but all too often they are very bloody and very long. I don't have the time to sit and wait. Who can say, this could be another like we fought with France."

"Which one?" asked Iain and the duke laughed.

"Are you sick?" she asked with concern.

"No. Not at all. Just know about men fighting is all. Don't make the mistake of thinking myself young, either. And here is your Mrs. O'Neal. Greetings, my lady." He caught Mrs. O'Neal's hand in his and kissed her knuckles. "I pray all is well with you?"

"That it is. Come sit in the dining room and I will bring you something. Tea?"

"Yes, that would be most welcome. Thank you."

"I will go and make sure the men get the carriage and horse tucked up right." Iain kissed Emily on the cheek and hurried off.

Emily and her grandfather were barely seated when Neddy came in, prompted by Mrs. O'Neal, Emily suspected. The last she had seen of the child he had been happily playing ball with the other boys. She watched as her grandfather hugged the boy and relaxed. Emily had feared he might turn away from Neddy as his heir because his father had not been gentry but she should have known better.

Iain came in and took the seat next to her. He was staring at her belly again and she was afraid he could see how it felt, which was a ridiculous thought, she scolded herself. Her belly was hidden behind a wide skirt and nobody could see what was happening with it, except for the fact that it had grown.

It was difficult but she held back a sound of surprise when the ache turned into a pain. "How was the journey then, Grandfather?"

"It was pleasant enough. The scenery is different enough, and plentiful enough to keep one's mind pleasantly occupied. We had no incidents and plentiful warnings about where any trouble was. We had a pretty uneventful journey. Ah, Malcolm did meet a rattler? I think that is what you call them."

"He was not bitten though, I hope."

"No. Screamed like a woman, however." He smiled when Emily laughed.

Mrs. O'Neal hurried in and started to put food on the table and a pot of tea. She next brought in coffee for Iain and a glass of apple cider for Neddy. When

Epilogue

It was utter chaos. Sam Connelly and Jackson Revannaugh stood over the barbecue grill on Alex and Georgina's back deck, arguing over what kind of barbecue rub was best for ribs.

Macy wore a princess crown and plastic high heels, clomping on the wooden deck like a wind-up toy learning to tap dance. Daniella, Amberly and Marjorie were setting the picnic table in the yard with colorful plasticware. Amberly's son Max was throwing a ball up in the air and catching it with a new catcher's mitt that Cole had bought for him.

Georgina mixed the dressing for a salad and watched out the window, reveling in the life that was happening among the people who had been captive for so long.

It had been six weeks since she'd left the hospital, eight weeks since they had all been released and Jacob Tanner had met his death.

This was the first time they had all joined together for a November picnic to celebrate the friendships that had formed through those long days and nights.

She finished with the dressing and moved on to

slicing tomatoes. As she worked, her head filled with thoughts of the past six weeks.

Magical. That was the only way she could describe her do-over with Alex. She'd started going to therapy immediately after getting out of the hospital, and each week with her therapist, she continued to exorcise her demons.

She had finally realized that she could trust Alex with her good and her bad, with her dreams and her heartaches, and in that trust they had found a new intimacy that Georgina had never thought possible, one that she had never experienced before.

The office snitch had been discovered to be a female cop who had leaked information both to the press and to Jacob Tanner. She was now facing charges of her own.

Georgina smiled as strong arms wrapped around her and she felt the solid presence of Alex just behind her. "Why aren't you out there playing with fire with Jackson and Sam?"

"Because I'm in here hugging you," he replied, his breath warm against her ear. He kissed her, nipping her earlobe playfully.

"Hmm, I think you might be playing with fire after all," she said. She pointed the knife she'd been using to slice tomatoes out the window. "I think we need one of those."

He stilled behind her, his arms tightening their embrace. "You mean, a tap-dancing princess?"

"Or a stick horse–riding cowboy." She set the knife down and turned in his arms.

His eyes glowed the impossible blue that always shot a wave of heat through her. "Really, Georgina?"

Emily made a move to help her the woman held her down with a firm hand on her shoulder.

"Shall I take something out for your men, Your Grace?" Mrs. O'Neal asked. "Or I can tell them to come on into the kitchen where I can feed them."

"If it would not be too much of a burden, I believe they would be quite pleased to eat in the kitchen. They have eaten outside or on the back of their horses for too long."

"One day we will have inns and such along the way, like the civilized countries. Well, after these fools are done killing each other," she muttered as she went to call in the duke's men.

Her grandfather watched Mrs. O'Neal leave with a half smile on his face. "Women do have their way of reducing all men to utter rubbish."

"It is a gift," said Emily. "And 'fools' is the right word. I have the awful feeling that at the very bottom of all the talk of rights and loyalty and so forth, it comes down to money. In the open it is one side demands something and will not bend and the other demands they see their side of things and will not bend. I call that idiocy."

The duke nodded. "It is. It is also the ways most wars begin. And the people who do not care either way are caught in the middle. The money? Quite possible, it is usually at the root of everything bad. At least this time it is not us."

"I did hear one man talking about the French helping the Rebs though." Iain looked at the duke. "Others say the English are helping. Even Spain is dipping its toe in the water."

"All those countries that would love to see this country brutally wound itself so they can, perhaps, slide right back into it."

"They'd never get in. Too many of us running about armed. Will be less soon, sad to say. If the listing of the dead after a battle is any indication it will be a lot less. Bloody slaughterhouse. And ye have to watch what ye say depending on where ye are, because showing any sympathy for the wrong side in the wrong place is a killing offense." Iain shook his head. "Idiots are destroying what they had, what most of the people like me would die for. A place where you can own your own land, put your own house on it, no matter who ye are. Just pay for it and it is all yours."

"And no lords to rule over you."

"No offense meant, Your Grace," said Iain. "But what man doesnae want to be free of all that?"

"None. In fact, my own men who have been at my side for years are casting a longing look at the places we go through as we come here. I pay well, too," he added with a grin.

"Ye would let them go, aye?"

"Of course. If nothing else, what good is a man who no longer wants the job but is held by tradition or lack of choice." He waved his hand. "You got out although I wish that damn idiot woman had offered a choice instead of tossing out a whole family."

"Weel, ye tossed her and her whole family out, I hear."

"Did not want that nasty business connected to the Stanton name. I may have whispered a word or two about what had been done in a sympathetic ear as well."

"Grandfather, you did not get her banished from society, did you?"

"Of course not. Just felt it should be known why

the family is disowned. No harm in that." He helped himself to some of the eggs and ham on the table.

"Sneaky."

"Probably but one must allow we old folks our little pleasures." He ate some of Mrs. O'Neal's excellent scrambled eggs. "My men must be in heaven right now sitting in a warm kitchen eating food like this. Malcolm might even forgive me for dragging him to someplace where they have such things as rattlers."

"Is he one who ye think is thinking of coming here or wishing on it?" asked Iain, who helped himself to a piece of ham.

"I think so but that may have changed his thinking."

"Why? Rattlers here. Adders in England," said Emmy. "Every place has its snake in the garden. This place might just have more but because it has not been settled for hundreds upon hundreds of years. So, people have not killed all the things they do not like."

"True and surprisingly cynical for you, Emmy. Have you found something you do not like here then?"

"Well, winter can be more brutal than I like but I have a house and fireplaces. Wolves grab his lambs but Iain has put up a fence and keeps a close watch. The vastness. And I have not found a solution for that yet."

"The vastness?" Her grandfather frowned and ate his eggs. "You are right. That is hard to adjust to and if it matters as to getting goods or having friends, even more so." He frowned and looked at her. "Emmy? You looked pained and startled. A very odd combination."

"Can you get Mrs. O'Neal, Iain?" she asked quietly, not sure how there was any way she could get out of the awkward position she now found herself in with any grace at all.

"Mrs. O'Neal!" bellowed Iain, and Neddy nearly fell out of his chair he was giggling so hard.

Emily rolled her eyes. "I could have done that."

"Then why didnae ye?"

The way he was watching her told her she was not hiding much at all from him. A glance at her grandfather said the same about him. There would be no slipping away with her wet skirts and not letting anyone know her water had broken. She would have to get to her bed soon though if the waves of pain rippling through her stomach were any clue.

Mrs. O'Neal came rushing in and ran to Emily's side. One quick glance told her what the problem was and she dashed off again. Iain was staring at the door the woman went through as if she had suddenly had a fit of madness but then Mrs. O'Neal came with a thick robe and a handful of towels. Helping Emily to her feet, Mrs. O'Neal yanked the robe on her, and then dropped the towels on the floor. Emily sighed. It would help with the mess but it certainly was not going to help save her dignity.

"Come along, dear, we will get you out to your room," Mrs. O'Neal said after linking her arm through Emily's. "Iain, put some water on to heat."

"What for? I want it born, not cooked. Ow!" he yelped when Mrs. O'Neal slapped him upside the head.

"For keeping things clean. Now git."

"Em?" said Neddy.

"She is going to have that bairn, lad. I can call ye when she is ready for ye to see it, if ye want."

"Yes, please. I will go play with Rory now." Neddy ran out of the house and Iain went into the kitchen.

Carrying his cup of tea, the duke followed Iain into the kitchen and sat at the table as Iain heated water. "I do believe Mrs. O'Neal is one of the reasons we cling so hard to our system."

Iain laughed and sat at the table opposite the duke. "Quite probably. She was what we needed when we got here about twelve years ago. But she needed us, too, and this place. Took one look at my stockade and decided that was the perfect spot for a new widow and her three bairns. By the time she had been here a year we had built her and the kids that cabin."

"Why the stockade?"

"Safety. I had lost enough people. I wanted walls, rather like a castle has, to hide me and my brothers behind."

"And now your wife and child."

"Children. Keep Neddy safe, too, Your Grace."

"Call me Harold. This is America, after all. You know I want the boy for my heir."

"I do but I think that has to be his choice and he is too young to make such a choice now."

"Agreed. No harm in me slowly easing him into knowing what the job entails, is there?"

"Nay. I just dinnae want him, weel, coerced into something he really hasnae got the heart for."

"Nor do I. I want the heart for the dukedom as well as the brain and brawn. And the stomach because he will always be the son of the blacksmith's son to society. He can never take that away, can never do anything to change that in people's minds. Wrong but that is how it is and he needs to know those things. I am not one who will be popping over on every holiday and birthday."

"I ken it. I just need to keep a watch on him." He leaned forward and met the duke's eye. "Ye see, Harold, the boy has the heart. He had a demmed big heart and your class, your society is a cruel lot. I dinnae think ye would disagree with that."

"Not at all."

"And I dinnae want the boy dragged into anything that will kill that sweetness in him."

"Agreed. Perhaps when he is older there can be a visit made. You or Emily or both of you can come over with him."

Realizing he was curious about how she had lived over there, Iain nodded, then tensed when a cry came from upstairs. "Emily."

"Son," Harold said as Iain lifted the pot of water, "you best get hardened to that sound because there will be a lot of them before that baby comes out. But you will have a fine son."

"Daughter. I am having a daughter."

"God help the poor child," murmured the duke.

He raced off to the kitchen and into the new rooms he and Emily had only to realize Mrs. O'Neal would have taken her into the sickroom. Cursing, he turned and ran back through the kitchen, past the duke, who was climbing the stairs and into the sickroom. The sight of Emily clinging to Mrs. O'Neal hand and panting made him lose some of his terror. She looked hale enough to him.

He set the water down and went to sit on the other side of Emily. She smiled at him but it was a tired expression and he had to wonder if she had the strength to go through with this. She took his hand in hers and held on so tight he hissed, then he changed his mind about her strength.

It went on for what felt like days to Emily and she hoped the women were right when they said you did not remember anything about the pain and mess afterward. Then the time came to push and she was so afraid she was simply too weary. Suddenly her grandfather was seated at the side of the bed holding her hand.

"Come on, child, you are a Stanton. It is time for the finale," he said, and smiled when she giggled, then just gently squeezed her hand and sat there.

Emily worked hard and began to think her child was as stubborn as its father. Between pushes she was all too aware of the various parts of her that were hurting. She looked up into the steel-gray eyes of her grandfather and grit her teeth. She would not fail the man. A glance at Iain made her determined to get the baby out before her poor husband disgraced himself with a swoon.

The newest MacEnroy made an entrance after taking far too long as far as Emily was concerned. Mrs. O'Neal let out a load guffaw and held up the baby to reveal a girl. Iain whooped and danced around the room.

"What are you doing?" asked Emily as soon as she had been cleaned off, and the covers pulled up. Then she held her arms out for her child and nearly wept when she was placed there by a beaming Mrs. O'Neal.

"I am doing a jig. I have broken the curse."

"What curse?"

"That the MacEnroys, our little twig of the clan, will never see a lass borne to them."

"That is one they usually use to curse one against having sons, not daughters."

"Some long-winded tale of love lost and an angry suitor, I suspect," said the duke. "I would like to loudly say nay, but, aye, that was pretty much the way of it."

"Well, jig your backside out and tell your brothers. With all the racket you have been making, they could be running up here soon." She laughed when he grinned at her, kissed her cheek and the baby's, and actually jigged out the door.

Emily was ready to sleep by the time all of Iain's brothers marched in and stared at the girl as if she was a mirage. "Did you never have a girl child born?"

"Sure, a lot of them in the broader clan but nay in our wee family. We had eight uncles and each of them got wed and had sons. The uncles claimed all they had had was uncles, too, and their father before them and on back. What is her name?"

"Nuala," Iain said. "Nuala Isbeal MacEnroy." All the brothers nodded solemnly as if giving him the last permission he needed to name his child after their mother.

Matthew reached out and lightly stroked the surprising mop of pale blond hair the child had. "Do ye think she will have your eyes, Iain, or yours, Emily?"

"She should have the Stanton steel eyes." The duke winked at Emily. "Emily softened them a bit but I forgive her. She is beautiful." He lightly touched the child's hair. "You did good."

Emily laughed but knew she would be falling asleep soon. By the time Iain cleared out the room she was barely able to keep her eyes open. Iain lay down beside her and kissed her cheek, then kissed little Nuala's.

"Thank ye, love. Thank ye for this precious gift."

"It is a gift to myself, too. I just hope I do not have to work so hard for any other gifts. It pleased your brothers that you named her after your mother."

"Aye. It has been a long time since a MacEnroy son could honor his mither in such a way. Shall I put her in her cradle?"

Emily stared at her child for a moment, kissed the top of her head, and handed her over to her father. She watched as Iain put the child in the cradle. Nuala Isbeal MacEnroy was going to need a dragon for a mother because every male in the family would be putty in her tiny hands. When Iain got back in bed, Emily curled up in his arms.

"I love ye, Emily Stanton," Iain whispered against her ear.

"A whole lot?"

"Ye cannae measure it."

"Enough to change her nappies all the time?"

He lifted his head to stare at her and, even though her eyes were closed, she was smiling. "Wretched woman. Nay. Some of the time, as when ye have a raging fever or a broken leg."

Emily tucked her face up against his neck, muttered something about it being worth a try, and fell asleep. Iain looked down at her and smiled. She was not very big but she could do mighty things. His brothers loved her like the sister they had never been blessed with and he was not sure she even realized that.

He looked toward the cradle to see his daughter sleeping and glanced up at the ceiling with a grin. If any woman had deserved the honor of having her name carried on it had been his mother. She had been both fierce when necessary and gentle when needed. He planned to see their daughter learned the same.

He called a duke by his Christian name and had a nephew who might become a duke.

He had conquered the enemy, insane fool that he was. Married a woman he loved. And still had his brothers at his side, annoying though they could be. All in all, he thought as he let sleep creep over him, he had had a great couple of years and, with Emily at his side, he planned on having many more.

More by Bestselling Author
Hannah Howell

"Really."

"We have one little issue to take care of first," he said.

"Just tell me when and where, and instead of do-over I'll say I do."

He grabbed her close and took her mouth in a fiery heat of possession. Tears of happiness misted her eyes as she tasted the complete and unconditional love in his kiss.

He finally broke the kiss and gazed at her with a tenderness she felt in her heart. "As soon as possible," he replied. "I want you as my wife again."

"And I want to be your wife again, but first we have a picnic to enjoy with new friends."

"And maybe later tonight we'll start on that little princess or cowboy," he said, and once again he captured her lips in a kiss that told her that this was the man of her heart, the man who would be at her side till the end of time.

* * * * *

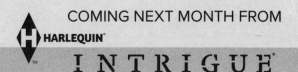
#1527 RUSTLING UP TROUBLE
Sweetwater Ranch • by Delores Fossen
Deputy Rayanne McKinnon believes ATF agent Blue McCurdy, father to
her unborn child, is dead—until he shows up with hired killers on his trail
and no memory of their night together.

#1528 THE HUNK NEXT DOOR
The Specialists • by Debra Webb & Regan Black
Fearless Police Chief Abigail Jensen seized a drug shipment, halting
the cash flow of an embedded terrorist cell. Can undercover specialist
Riley O'Brien find the threat before the terrorists retaliate?

#1529 BONEYARD RIDGE
The Gates • by Paula Graves
To save her from a deadly ambush, undercover P.I. Hunter Bragg takes
Susannah Marsh on the run. But when their escape alerts a dangerous
enemy from Susannah's past, Hunter will need to rely on the other
members of The Gates to rescue the woman who healed his heart.

#1530 CROSSFIRE CHRISTMAS
The Precinct • by Julie Miller
When injured undercover cop Charlie Nash kidnapped nurse
Teresa Rodriguez to stitch up his wounds, he never meant to put his
brave rescuer in danger...or fall in love with her.

#1531 COLD CASE AT COBRA CREEK
by Rita Herron
Someone in town will do anything to stop Sage Freeport from getting the
truth about her missing son. Tracker Dugan Graystone's offer to help is
Sage's best chance to find her child...and lose her heart....

#1532 NIGHT OF THE RAVEN
by Jenna Ryan
When an old curse is recreated by someone seeking revenge, only
Ethan McVey, the mysterious new Raven's Cove police chief, stands
between Amara Bellam and a brutal killer.

REQUEST YOUR FREE BOOKS!
2 FREE NOVELS PLUS 2 FREE GIFTS!

⊕HARLEQUIN®
INTRIGUE®

BREATHTAKING ROMANTIC SUSPENSE

YES! Please send me 2 FREE Harlequin Intrigue® novels and my 2 FREE gifts (gifts are worth about $10). After receiving them, if I don't wish to receive any more books, I can return the shipping statement marked "cancel." If I don't cancel, I will receive 6 brand-new novels every month and be billed just $4.74 per book in the U.S. or $5.24 per book in Canada. That's a savings of at least 14% off the cover price! It's quite a bargain! Shipping and handling is just 50¢ per book in the U.S. and 75¢ per book in Canada.* I understand that accepting the 2 free books and gifts places me under no obligation to buy anything. I can always return a shipment and cancel at any time. Even if I never buy another book, the two free books and gifts are mine to keep forever.

182/382 HDN F42N

Name _____ (PLEASE PRINT)

Address _____ Apt. #

City _____ State/Prov. _____ Zip/Postal Code

Signature (if under 18, a parent or guardian must sign)

Mail to the **Harlequin® Reader Service:**
IN U.S.A.: P.O. Box 1867, Buffalo, NY 14240-1867
IN CANADA: P.O. Box 609, Fort Erie, Ontario L2A 5X3
**Are you a subscriber to Harlequin Intrigue books and want to receive the larger-print edition?
Call 1-800-873-8635 or visit www.ReaderService.com.**

* Terms and prices subject to change without notice. Prices do not include applicable taxes. Sales tax applicable in N.Y. Canadian residents will be charged applicable taxes. Offer not valid in Quebec. This offer is limited to one order per household. Not valid for current subscribers to Harlequin Intrigue books. All orders subject to credit approval. Credit or debit balances in a customer's account(s) may be offset by any other outstanding balance owed by or to the customer. Please allow 4 to 6 weeks for delivery. Offer available while quantities last.

Your Privacy—The Harlequin® Reader Service is committed to protecting your privacy. Our Privacy Policy is available online at www.ReaderService.com or upon request from the Harlequin Reader Service.

We make a portion of our mailing list available to reputable third parties that offer products we believe may interest you. If you prefer that we not exchange your name with third parties, or if you wish to clarify or modify your communication preferences, please visit us at www.ReaderService.com/consumerschoice or write to us at Harlequin Reader Service Preference Service, P.O. Box 9062, Buffalo, NY 14269. Include your complete name and address.

HI13R

SPECIAL EXCERPT FROM

 HARLEQUIN®

INTRIGUE

*A surprise attack on her family ranch reunites a pregnant
deputy with her baby's father—who supposedly died five
months ago...*

Read on for an excerpt from
RUSTLING UP TROUBLE
by USA TODAY *bestselling author*

Delores Fossen

She put her hand on his back to steady him. Bare skin on
bare skin.

The hospital gown hardly qualified as a garment, with
one side completely off his bandaged shoulder. Judging
from the drafts he felt on various parts of his body, Rayanne
was probably getting an eyeful.

Of course, it apparently wasn't something she hadn't
already seen, since according to her they'd slept together
five months ago.

"Will saying I'm sorry help?" he mumbled, and because
he had no choice, he ditched the bargaining-position idea
and lay back down.

"Nothing will help. As soon as you're back on your feet,
I want you out of Sweetwater Springs and miles and miles
away from McKinnon land. Got that?"

Oh, yeah. It was crystal clear.

It didn't matter that he didn't know why he'd done the
things he had, but he'd screwed up. Maybe soon, Blue would
remember everything that he might be trying to forget.

HIEXP69794

Her phone rang, the sound shooting through the room. And his head. Rayanne fished the phone from her pocket, looked at the screen and then moved to the other side of the room to take the call. It occurred to him then that she might be involved with someone.

Five months was a long time.

And this someone might be calling to make sure she was okay.

Blue felt the twinge of jealousy that throbbed right along with the pain in various parts of his body, and he wished he could just wake up from this crazy nightmare that he was having.

"No, he doesn't remember," she said to whoever had called. She turned to look back at him, but her coat shifted to the side.

Just enough for Blue to see the stomach bulge beneath her clothes.

Oh, man.

It felt as if someone had sucked the air right out of his lungs. He didn't need his memory to understand what that meant.

Rayanne was pregnant.

Find out how Rayanne reacts to Blue's discovery and what they plan to do to protect their unborn child when
RUSTLING UP TROUBLE
by USA TODAY bestselling author
Delores Fossen hits shelves in November 2014.

HARLEQUIN®

I N T R I G U E

A NATIVE AMERICAN TRACKER MAKES IT HIS MISSION TO BRING HOME A MISSING CHILD JUST IN TIME FOR CHRISTMAS...

After two years, Sage Freeport had all but given up hope of seeing her little boy again...until she met Dugan Graystone. They shared a disdain for local law enforcement, the same folks who'd hindered Sage's efforts to find her son. As an expert tracker, the broad-shouldered Native American was sure he could find the child—even if he had to leave Texas to do it. Spending time with Sage, watching as she broke down every time a lead didn't pan out, Dugan worked harder than he ever had before. Now, with Christmas just days away, Dugan knew Sage trusted him to give her the greatest gift of all: bring Benji home....

COLD CASE AT COBRA CREEK

BY RITA HERRON

Only from Harlequin® Intrigue®.
Available November 2014
wherever books and ebooks are sold.

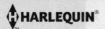

HARLEQUIN®

INTRIGUE®

READ THE FINAL INSTALLMENT OF
JULIE MILLER'S GRIPPING MINISERIES
THE PRECINCT: TASK FORCE

With his life bleeding out from bullet wounds and a car crash, Charles Nash's best option is to kidnap the innocent nurse who stops to help him. At gunpoint, the jaded DEA undercover agent offers Teresa Rodriguez a desperate deal: if she keeps him alive long enough to find out who's blown his cover and set him up to die, she'll be home for Christmas.

But can he keep that promise?

As the two go on the run from an unknown killer, the Good Samaritan gives Nash a bad case of unprofessional desire. He's drawn to the sexy little spitfire for her bravery, boldness and attitude. But he won't count on kissing her under mistletoe. The cartel thugs after Nash want them both dead!

CROSSFIRE CHRISTMAS
BY JULIE MILLER

Only from Harlequin® Intrigue®.
Available November 2014
wherever books and ebooks are sold.

U E®

SIGNMENT
GATOR
URE.
BUT ONLY IF HE CAN KEEP
SUSANNAH MARSH ALIVE.

All Hunter Bragg wanted in Purgatory, Tennessee, was a
little peace of mind. A private investigator plagued by his
own guilt, he never imagined his next job would resurrect
old demons. Targeted by an anarchistic militia group,
events planner Susannah Marsh is his next mission: keep
her close…keep her alive. But Susannah has a secret.
A secret that will reveal the true motive of her potential
assailants. For Hunter, being Susannah's protector soon
becomes more than just a job. And in order to succeed,
there can be no half measures. With undeniable attraction
simmering between them, he's determined not to let
the promise of a better future fall into the hands
of ruthless predators.

BONEYARD RIDGE
by PAULA GRAVES

Only from Harlequin® Intrigue®.
Available November 2014
wherever books and ebooks are sold.

m

HI69796